AF508191

MOUNTAINS
OF OUR
OWN

MOUNTAINS
OF OUR
OWN

*A Teen's Journey to
Find Her Gift*

DELANEY KRAEMER

EDITED BY DAVID ARETHA

Published by Neurodivergent Publications

For more information or to contact the author, visit
http://neurodivergentpublications.com/

Edited by David Aretha
Book cover design by Alissa J. Zavalianos, A to Z Cover Design
Book interior design by Jesse Gordon, A Darned Good Book

ISBN (paperback): 979-8-9886657-0-0
ISBN (hardcover): 979-8-9886657-1-7
ISBN (ebook): 979-8-9886657-2-4

Library of Congress Control Number: 2023914026

Printed in the United States of America

Dedication

To all with a medical condition and those who are neurodivergent.

Prologue

Ten years earlier

Labeled boxes of toys were scattered throughout the classroom, and bookshelves lined a section of the room. Mats with colorful numbers and a carpet depicting a highway covered the floor. Echoes of rippling, bubbly laughter resounded.

"Have a great day, sweetheart. Go join the others." Mom kissed her five-year-old daughter as she left the classroom. Faith giggled as she galloped toward the other students, who encircled the alphabet carpet.

That afternoon, the children were permitted to play with the toys or read the books from the shelves—this was Faith's favorite time of the school day.

Caleb was jumping and whirling around the room. "Sit down, Caleb," the kindergarten teacher instructed.

Meanwhile, Faith was busy looking at a picture book at a table. Grace soon joined Faith. She placed the doll with which she was playing on the rectangular table while she was busy doing a craft.

"Excuse me, can I borrow that green crayon?" asked Grace with a bounce of her golden ringlets. She smiled, her big, blue eyes shimmering.

"Yes," Faith said. Errant strands of her fiery, red ponytails were flying everywhere. She had a peachy skin tone.

Gabe came over and asked, "What are you reading?"

"This," Faith said and showed him. Gabe had shaggy, light hair, a round face, intelligent-looking wide eyes, and dimples.

"Nice," Gabe chuckled as he grinned, showing his two missing front teeth.

"Hey," Caleb said as he bounded toward them. He ruffled his long, wild, bushy, black hair. "I went to basketball today! The coach said I did a good job."

"Good job!" Faith echoed.

"I was so hungry! That yogurt was delicious," Caleb said.

"I just lost my two front teeth. I've been waiting forever," Gabe said proudly, as he laughed.

"I'm still waiting for mine to fall out. I like to lose teeth, because the tooth fairy comes and gives me coins," Caleb responded.

"Nap time!" announced the teacher.

After five minutes, all the kids settled down and got cozy on their pillows and sleep mats.

Her eyes fluttering open, Faith woke up to the feeling of pain in her limbs. She convulsed, her legs and arms tightening and releasing. But soon she lost consciousness.

Gabe sat up to find Faith groaning and jerking uncontrollably beside him. Grace, Caleb, Gabe, and the other students gathered in a little huddle around Faith, whose eyes were rolled back.

"Is she okay?" Gabe asked softly.

"Hold on. Faith, can you hear me?" the teacher asked. "I think she's having a seizure. We need to call an ambulance and Faith's parents."

Gabe was terror-stricken and was frozen next to Faith.

"Gabe, you need to get away from there!" Grace cried out.

"What's happening?" Gabe asked. "I want my mom."

"Me, too," Grace whimpered.

Chapter One

Present day

Fifteen-and-a-half-year-old Faith adjusted her crossbody bag as she made her way out of the girls' bathroom.

Faith had brown freckles scattered across her nose and cheeks. The late afternoon sunlight gave a luster to Faith's bright, fiery, red hair that was wild with waves. She had warm brown eyes.

Teens' voices echoed through the hallways of St. Gianna High School. It was August, the beginning of the school year. Faith's best friend, Grace, waved her over to the line of kids, who were flowing out of the auditorium from drama club. Faith only came to Grace's school on Thursday afternoons. Faith had epilepsy, and so she had to sleep for about fifteen hours a day. One of Faith's doctors explained to her that the brain recovers from the relentless seizure activity during sleep. Since she couldn't get up early, Faith was homeschooled.

Grace was scanning the bulletin board beside her on the wall. "Faith, Mr. Perry said at the meeting today that he wants us members to come up with ideas for the next play! You should totally sign up for one of the roles!" Grace cried with a bounce of her blond curls as she turned her head.

"I've never had a role before," Faith worried. "What if my brain glitches and I forget my lines? What if I can't come to the practices because of my sleeping schedule?"

"My best friend is never a quitter." Grace swung her arm. Her gleaming blue eyes beseeched Faith.

"Fine, I'll sign up," groaned Faith, her shoulders slumping.

"Hey, girls!" Gabe said and high-fived Faith. He fist-bumped Grace. Gabe was Faith's close friend; he also happened to be Grace's fifteen-year-old cousin.

Gabe, studying Faith's face, observed, "What's wrong? Are you sick?"

"Yes. It's only nausea from seizure, but it will go away soon," Faith reassured calmly as she put her hand to her chest.

"It's also something else," Gabe said and looked down at her legs, as he saw the left one jerk for a second.

"It's just jerking," Faith said while she tried to sound calm.

"What does it feel like?" Gabe asked with curiosity. He wore a saddened expression.

"My leg gets really tense and sore. I also have tingling in my limbs. My arms are also tight," Faith explained.

"I'm sorry," said Gabe sympathetically.

"It's all right; I'll just ignore it like I always do." Faith chuckled uneasily as she faked a smile.

"Does it help if you take deep breaths?" offered Gabe.

"No, nothing helps," Faith responded. She was dizzy and had a seizure-induced feeling to cry. She felt like she was going to tip over. Just then, Faith's phone alarm went off.

"What is that alarm for?" Gabe inquired casually. His hands were in his pants pockets.

"My afternoon pill," Faith responded as she got her big phone out of her backpack's side pocket. She swiped the alarm off. "One moment, let me just find a water fountain..." Faith turned to go, and in the middle of the hall she stopped. One glance told Grace what was going on with her best friend.

"The fog is taking over," Grace explained.

"The what?" Gabe asked, confused.

"It means that she's having trouble thinking. Faith told me that when it happens, it feels as though a fog is over her head," defined Grace.

"What was I about to do? I was finding something..." Puzzled, Faith looked at the floor as she thought for a moment.

"The water fountain. Here, I'll walk you there," Gabe obliged as he walked toward her.

Faith pushed past the nausea and dizziness as she strode toward the fountain with Gabe at her side. The tingling tickled her leg and then it jerked. She thanked Gabe for going with her. A burning electric feeling slowly made its way up the back of her head while Faith waved a goodbye to Gabe. She was nauseated as she sipped the water. She forced herself to ignore the nausea.

"Hey," Grace said, "I'm so happy to suggest a play. I—" Faith heard murmuring and words coming out of Grace's mouth, but the words were quickly forgotten as soon as she heard them. The nausea was overpowering, and her head prickled for a moment, and then it ceased.

"What did you say? I don't remember," Faith asked.

"Oh, I was just saying about how happy I feel to be part of such an amazing club," beamed Grace. She folded her hands at her middle as she laughed.

"Me, too." Faith smiled as her headache pulsed.

"And I was about to say I'm excited to suggest a play," Grace remarked.

Grace saw Faith's right arm jerk and was filled with compassion.

"Come on, let's get ice cream at TCBY! That'll cheer you up!" Grace said and motioned for her friend to follow her.

Before the Whistle Blows

Poofy steam came from the textile mill whistle at 5:30 a.m. Pale blue, light pink, and faint orange painted the sky as the sun began to rise. It was a misty morning in New York at the farm in May 1910.

Mark poured a pitcher of water, which was from the stream that was behind the house, into a ceramic bowl. In addition to the stream water, Mark added the precious soap flakes. Closing his gentle blue eyes tightly to shield himself from the freezing cold water, Mark splashed soapy water across his hot, oily face. Immediately, he submerged his head into the water and raked his fingers through his sweat-soaked, curly, cream-colored hair. He scrubbed his broad shoulders and scrawny arms. Mark then pulled on his mended stockings and brown leather boots that had lost their shine. They had holes in them, and most of their buttons were missing. He pulled on his britches, suspenders, outgrown blazer, and newsboy cap. Looking at his reflection in the smeared and cracked mahogany, octagon-shaped mirror, Mark quickly shaved off his dark, golden, bristly whiskers. His grandmother had given the mirror to his pa and ma when they married.

Sitting alone at the kitchen table, Mark wolfed down his breakfast of porridge. Afterward, he helped his younger siblings, who served as farmhands, with their chores of gathering eggs, milking the goats, and feeding the animals.

With a lunch pail swinging by his side, Mark headed to the big city toward the textile mill. Walking past the tall, suited men in bowler and boater hats, Mark avoided the wagon horses' dung on the dirt road and meandered around ladies in plumed, floral, elaborate hats. Hawking newsboys lined the streets. At the same time, little boys in their corner of the streets shined the citizens' leather shoes. The middle-class customers were sitting on their throne-like, wooden chairs towering over the laborers. Young boys in woolen uniforms, who were delivering mail, whizzed by on their bicycles with saggy book bags slugged over their shoulders. Little girls with bows in their hair, clothed in plain frocks, and boys in tweed britches, waistcoats, and blazers, walked in a straight procession together toward the school-house, carrying their books with them.

Some boys and girls were fortunate not to have to work. Mark wished he could go to school and learn how to read, but he didn't have the time, and Mama didn't have the money. Mark came upon the familiar, secluded dirt path that looked like it had a dusty orange glow from the dawn.

"Hello, Mark," Mary galloped toward him. Her black hair was up in a loose bun with uneven locks hanging out. Sunlight, which was just on the horizon, glistened on her oil-stained work smock.

"Oh, hello, Mary. What happened to your hair?" Mark asked, alarmed that her hair was cut unevenly and had strands that were longer or shorter than the others.

Mary wore a stained, loose, puffy-sleeved frock under her smock. Her dark stockings and the skirt of her smock were covered in lint, dirt, and oil. She had an oval-shaped face, fine eyebrows, glimmering, plaintive gray eyes, and an upturned nose. Light purple circles were evident under her eyes.

"Oh, The Overlooker cut it as a consequence of my conversing with you," Mary explained as they approached the large, brick building with big, glass-paneled windows that were never opened. Glossy ivy climbed the brick and across the vertical line of windows.

"That's terrible. I wish he wouldn't do such a thing to you," Mark commented. "I wonder what The Overlooker will be using today—his strap or his trusty stick?" he grumbled, looking down at his boots. He raised his eyes toward the entrance of the textile mill. They had arrived at the building.

"I'll speak to you at luncheon, Mark," Mary said as she went toward the other girl workers. Mark was filled with disappointment; he hated that they couldn't talk more often.

"You're late!" shouted an all-too-familiar voice that set Mark on edge.

"Hello, Mr. John," said Mark.

"You know what being late means, don'cha?" asked the cocky overlooker, his leather strap in his hand. Mark still shuddered, even though he was used to the sight of the strap. The overlooker took his leather strap and beat Mark till his back dribbled with maroon-shaded blood. Mark was in anguish, but he knew the overlooker took pleasure in inflicting pain on him, so he bit down on his bottom lip until he tasted blood. Mark pressed his lips together and clenched his jaws. Sweat beaded down his forehead as he bent over.

There's going to be several welts tomorrow morning, thought Mark.

"Get to work!" the overlooker yelled.

Mary was a couple feet away on the left side of the room, checking for loose threads on the bobbins with the other girl spinners. She gasped in shock when she saw Mark's bloodied back; her eyes welled up with tears.

The doffers replaced the bobbins in the machine and slid, barefoot, across the oily floor. Their cheeks were hot from the humid temperature, as they worked diligently on the same repetitive tasks. As the hours passed, the room grew more stifling; Mark and Mary perspired as their knees shook beneath them.

The whistle blew for lunch at noon.

Standing near the machines and talking to Mark, Mary held an oat cake in one hand and was eating it intermittently.

Mary explained to Mark, saying, "My sister's walking now."

"I have a great fondness in my heart for your young sister. She's so precious," Mark chuckled, standing beside her.

"I have a deep tenderness for her as well," smiled Mary.

After lunch, everyone went back to their bone-tiring work. Hours later, Mark reached up toward the spinning frame of the power looms as he heard the deafening, rhythmic noise of the machines and the shuttles. Mary wheezed while she gazed out of the closed windows. She breathed in the dusty and linty air of the mill. Mary got any lint out of the bobbins as she concentrated, while the machines proceeded to work. The thread was stretched way out, woven around and around, and then brought back with a clank. Little children were on all fours, brushing clumps of lint from the floor as the machines functioned. The boys of five, six, and seven got up for a moment—splinters, calluses, and deep bruises on their knobby knees.

Mark pulled a handful of bobbins that had tightly wrapped woolen thread around them. After taking them off, he placed an armful in a wicker basket. He then replaced the machine with new, empty bobbins.

At six o'clock the whistle blew, telling everyone to go home. They had done their twelve hours of work.

Chapter Two

Grace's mother drove her daughter and Faith to TCBY, their favorite frozen yogurt shop.

Mrs. Foster's soft, cream-colored curls draped over her shoulders. She had blue-green eyes that had wrinkles beneath them.

Faith took a few spoonfuls of her chocolate ice cream. She abruptly felt nauseated and sunk into her seat. She heaved a sigh and said, "I'm sick; I can't eat anymore."

A few minutes later, Faith leaned forward to eat her ice cream again, because the nausea was gone. It came back moments later. She ate some ice cream and sucked on it, as she waited for the overpowering nausea to stop. Her left arm felt tight.

"I was thinking about the play we're supposed to come up with. How about we suggest *The Miracle Worker*? Oh, fun fact—actually, it's not kinda fun. Did you know Kate Keller wouldn't let Helen Keller marry her one true love, Fagan, because she had challenges? Silly, right?" Grace scoffed, making fun over Helen's family's ignorance. "After all they did to help her learn to communicate and to be independent! It would've been actually good for Helen to be happy and have children and a husband."

"Oh, Helen Keller! I learned about her! I think she was a genius. She knew multiple languages, and graduated with honors in college. But she struggled with math. She was very dedicated to getting things right, and was a perfectionist. She had deafness and blindness. Did you even know that Helen was an activist for people with challenges?" Faith added.

"Do you know if she was born with deafness and blindness?" Grace asked.

"No, she wasn't born with it. At nineteen months, she got really sick with scarlet fever or meningitis. It was a miracle that she got well. Sadly, it left her with a hurt brain. She couldn't hear or see. She was perfectly healthy except for her absent senses."

"I heard Helen got really angry all the time since she couldn't communicate. Then, Annie Sullivan came and taught her how to sign in people's hands," Grace explained.

"I wish I could be more proficient at signing. My motor skills are terrible." Faith frowned down at her fist.

"Helen was pretty with her sky-blue eyes and golden chestnut hair. I colored her childhood pictures on my coloring app when I was younger."

After a short hesitation, Grace pointed out, saying, "Hey, are you feeling better?"

"Yes, I'm feeling better, and I'm just pushing through it," Faith responded.

"Oh, okay," Grace nodded.

* * *

The next week, Faith went back to her friends' school. It was still perfect summer weather—balmy and cloudless, and the grass was lush.

Faith's eyes adjusted to the dim auditorium as she took her seat next to Grace and Gabe. Gabe was laughing and telling jokes. The trio were waiting for drama club to start.

"How are you doing, Gabe?" Faith asked.

"Fine," replied Gabe.

"'Sup, Faith." Caleb bounded over. He patted Faith on the shoulder. He was like the brother that Faith never had.

Caleb raked his fingers through a thick piece of his hair that was standing up on end. He had a playful smile and wide-set hazel eyes that were always looking around.

"Welcome back, kiddos," Mr. Perry said. He wore a black, button-down shirt and black slacks. He had a round face and black stubble on his upper lip, neat brown hair, and bushy eyebrows. "Take a seat. I want to hear your suggestions on our next play. Thoughts?"

"How about we put on *Anastasia*?" a student suggested. Mr. Perry scribbled the title of the play on a whiteboard.

"*Dear Evan Hansen*," said a boy in the second row.

"That *is* a great musical, but the script just came out, and I don't know if I can get the licensing," Mr. Perry answered.

"*Les Miserables*?" asked a female student, and Mr. Perry wrote it down.

"How about *The Hunchback of Notre Dame*?" recommended another female student.

"*My Fair Lady*," a student called out.

"*Oklahoma*," another student said.

"*42nd Street*?" asked one student. "It's really jazzy."

"How about we put on *The Miracle Worker*, sir?" Grace offered.

"Yeah, I watched the movies and it seems really good. I've also watched different interpretations online," Faith agreed. Mr. Perry scrawled the title on his whiteboard along with all of the other titles.

"*The Secret Garden*?" Gabe asked. "My choir has been practicing the songs."

"*Shrek*! It has a lot of upbeat music, fun costumes, and lots of humor," Caleb grinned.

"*Fiddler on the Roof*," recommended a girl in the first row.

"Tradition!" a boy sang as he raised his arms, and snapped. Everyone laughed.

"You kids can all take a vote," Mr. Perry remarked.

Chapter Three

Mom had offered to pick up Gabe from choir, since Faith and Gabe were planning to hang out in the late afternoon.

The choir was singing "A Bit of Earth Reprise" from *The Secret Garden* when Mom and Faith entered. Some teens picked up their things to go home while others still chatted, waiting for their rides.

"Faith!" Gabe called over to her.

Soon, Gabe and Faith loaded into her mother's car. They passionately sang "You've Always Been" by Unspoken.

"Faith, how about we practice this song with the band?" Gabe asked.

Caleb, Grace, Faith, and Gabe enjoyed music and always wanted to be in a band together. As they grew older, they began to learn how to play instruments. They started to learn Christian songs, and the four of them formed a band that played at their church. Gabe and Faith sang Christian songs and listened to instrumentals all the way to Faith's house.

Mom stopped the van and Faith walked up the porch steps to the large brick house, using both handrails. She unlocked the white-painted front door.

The living room was dark blue with large windows, a fireplace, an oak-finished floor, and a white window seat. There was a bird feeder in front of the window.

"What are you working on, Gabe?" Faith asked as she poured two bowls of Doritos for them. They sat on the couch together.

"Nothing much. I've been practicing a 'True Colors' cover performed by Justin Timberlake and Anna Kendrick," Gabe responded as he smoothed back his shaggy, cream-colored hair.

"Oh, I love that song. It makes me sleepy," smiled Faith. She laughed softly. "Do you know what Mr. Perry chose for our next play?"

"I heard him say something about *The Miracle Worker*," Gabe answered, curling his legs beside him on the couch.

"Are you serious?" asked Faith excitedly.

"Yes," Gabe replied.

"Now, you're sure he's choosing *The Miracle Worker*?" Faith held up a hand.

"Pretty sure...." Gabe laughed. "Yeah...he told me after school this afternoon," confirmed Gabe with a grin.

"Really?" exclaimed Faith.

"Yes!" Gabe chuckled.

"I wish I could be Helen," Faith said longingly.

"You can try out for that role," Gabe encouraged. "I know you want it."

"I'm afraid I'll screw up," Faith said.

"Give it a try," Gabe said. "It couldn't hurt." Faith nodded and shrugged.

"Are you disappointed that the play's not *The Secret Garden*, though?" Faith asked gently.

"A little, but maybe we can do it next year," Gabe responded, reaching for a chip. "Did you know I'm taking a philosophy class?"

Faith beamed, saying, "I am *not* a fan of philosophy, but I love to think deeply. I don't want to have to memorize all the different philosophers and their different beliefs. I haven't studied it, but I like to contemplate religion. My personal philosophy? I think that you should just love God's creations and Him."

"True," Gabe shrugged. "I like to think deeply, too. Yeah, learning about all the different philosophers can be confusing, but it's interesting to learn."

"Maybe I just have to be more enthusiastic about learning it and learn it in a different way," Faith shrugged.

"Maybe I could help you," Gabe said. "I could give you fun facts and make it sound as exciting as much as it is to me."

"But do you like theology, too? It sounds up your alley," Faith asked.

"Actually, I do. Now that I've been a part of a philosophy class, I think I like theology better—you were spot on. I love reading Scripture—that's part of it. I like connecting to Jesus through it."

"Through theology?" Faith asked.

"No, through Scripture. Sorry, I wasn't clear," Gabe said.

"Do you want to study theology or philosophy in college? Like, get a degree in it?"

"Yeah, I think I want to pursue a career in theology—even like a college professor or something."

"You mean, you wanna teach? That's a tough job, and draining. Would you be satisfied with being a high school teacher?"

"Yeah, even if the job doesn't pay well, despite educating the future generations."

"You'd be really good at it," Faith said.

"I don't know—I like so many subjects, like biology and musical theater. So maybe I want to be a theater major, and get like a BFA, a Bachelor in Fine Arts, or study English, or linguistics, or science, or government...I don't know yet."

"You could go to the University of Michigan or University of Detroit," suggested Faith. "Or Sacred Heart Seminary."

"Maybe U of M or U of D, but I'm not sure about the seminary. At first, I thought about being a priest, but now I think I'm called to marriage."

"Well, you can take courses at the seminary without entering the priesthood," Faith said. "You'll figure it out."

"How about you?" asked Gabe.

"I'm not sure yet. Have you got any more ideas for yourself?" Faith asked.

"Way to deflect, Faith, and totally brush off the question!" Gabe exclaimed.

"It'd be cool to be a dialect coach or a language therapist," said Faith.

Faith let out a chortle, setting her right hand on the couch, using it to stabilize herself.

"Do you still like science?" Faith asked casually.

"I find it interesting," Gabe replied.

"Fascinating?" Faith continued. "I love biology, the hormones, the bones, the eyeballs, hair—stuff like that. But definitely not the cells. But I don't fully believe in evolution; I believe God made all that cool stuff."

Gabe smiled. "Cells are the building blocks of life, Faith." He laughed.

"Sorry, I misspoke. I mean, I don't like learning about the individual parts of cells, like mitochondria. It's boring."

"That's my classic, Faith. I'm happy that you like science, though. I like your ideas and the way you think."

"Even if they are wild and crazy— which I know they are," Faith chuckled. "And my obsessions with the early twentieth century, alongside my plain, practical clothes and hairstyles."

Gabe nodded approvingly. "You've got a unique style in music and clothing—that's for sure. Like, you're open to new customs and differences, you know?"

"Well, thanks....I think..." Faith looked puzzled.

"I've been wondering for a while: How did you end up loving Christian tunes?"

"God wanted me to find it, I guess," Faith shrugged. "I found Christian contemporary music when I was ten. I know they're popular with the Christian community. They're catchy and you can't really tell the difference between secular and religious pop."

"Yeah, they should play our Christian music on the radio, and nobody could tell the difference," Gabe said.

"We should start a petition! That was a joke if you couldn't tell," said Faith, winking.

"I don't know many teenagers who like the stuff you do. I think it's pretty cool," Gabe said. "Want to watch a movie?"

"Segue alert! Sure, what should we watch?" Faith asked.

"*Gifted*. That McKenna Grace is talented. When she cries, it wrenches my heart!" Gabe said.

Chapter Four

The next day, Caleb and Faith planned a day to hang out. Bounding out of the house, Faith walked down the porch steps as she gripped the handrails. Birdsong filled the air as Faith smelled sunshine and fresh breeze. She waved to Caleb, who was in the back seat of his family's SUV. Faith entered the car and buckled up.

I really hope I can feel better so I can have a good time with Caleb today. I don't want to feel miserable from seizures, Faith thought.

They drove to the mall because Mrs. Johnson needed to shop. On the way there, Caleb and Faith were singing to old classics like "My Girl," "Pretty Woman," "A Little Girl Named Jo," and "Rockin' Robin." They also listened to TobyMac and Jordan Feliz.

* * *

Groups of customers walked quickly from one shop to another in the mall. Their chatter echoed around Faith. She looked down at the twinkling, cream-colored, terrazzo tile.

Caleb inquired, "Mom, can we get a pretzel and a slushy?" He looked at Faith. "Do you want some?"

"No thanks, man," Faith declined.

"Sure, you can get a pretzel and a slushy," Mrs. Johnson shrugged. "But...um...you just ate."

Mrs. Johnson had short, shoulder-length, curly brown hair. She had round blue eyes, fair skin, and a nice smile. Her husband bragged to his co-workers that she was a dead ringer for Claire Foy.

Reaching for his wallet, Caleb offered, "But I can pay for it. I have some cash."

Faith breathed through her mouth as they passed the pretzel storefront.

"Want a bite?" Caleb asked as he gave Faith the package.

"No thanks, it smells foul, and I don't really like pretzels anyway." Faith scrunched her nose while she grimaced.

"Who doesn't like pretzels?" Caleb opened his mouth wide as he ate a big bite.

"Caleb really likes his junk food," Mrs. Johnson said as she smiled at him. "If I ate food like he does, I'd be a moose."

Caleb rolled his eyes.

"May we go to Claire's?" Faith pointed to the store.

"Do we have to?" whined Caleb.

"Hey, if you go, I won't ask you to go to Bath & Body Works," Faith said.

"Deal." Caleb shook her hand. "But let's make it quick."

"Don't worry. I'm a fast window shopper," joked Faith.

"Actually, I need to look for a gift for my sister at Bath & Body Works," Mrs. Johnson said. "Meet me there."

"No fair!" Caleb called after his mother.

In Claire's, Caleb tried on sunglasses for fun and made faces. He tried on the ones with hanging mustaches. Faith tried on a rose-gold pair that was heart-shaped. They exited Claire's and Caleb spotted a kiosk with motorized animals encircling it.

"Man! It's just like a motorcycle!" Caleb sprinted toward it. "Let's ride one!" He got a wad of cash out of his wallet.

"I don't know if we should ride on that," Faith said, a worried expression on her face.

"Come on, Faith. Who cares what other people think?" Caleb laughed. He handed the woman at the stand his money. The woman unplugged the zebra from its charging station and told Caleb how to work it. Caleb got on and waved Faith over.

"Come on! It's not bad!" grinned Caleb.

"Okay," Faith said nervously. She got onto the zebra behind Caleb, putting her arms around his waist. They propped their feet on the running board, as Caleb pressed the accelerator pedal with his foot.

"Dang it! It doesn't go as fast as I thought it would," Caleb remarked downheartedly.

"It's still fun," Faith said optimistically. "You can't have a speeding zebra in the mall. It'd be mayhem!"

Soon, they were back with Mrs. Johnson, who was at Bath & Body Works. She was sauntering through the aisles, scanning the products. Mrs. Johnson was gentle and elegant and a tenderhearted mother to Caleb.

"This is my jam!" shouted Caleb as he heard "Jump in Line" on the radio. He picked up a sparkly, tall, large perfume bottle. He sang into it as he did an arm wave and performed some samba dance steps. Faith and Mrs. Johnson exchanged a glance. It was apparent that Mrs. Johnson was blushing.

Trying to join in with her friend, Faith picked up a peach-scented perfume. But the whole tower fell down onto the floor like a stack of dominoes. Faith turned red as she, Mrs. Johnson, Caleb, and some employees picked up the mess.

Faith giggled as Caleb continued to dance. He laughed and beamed with delight.

Caleb was very secure in who he was. He didn't mind dancing in public—whether it was at the mall or the grocery store. He wasn't afraid to be his brazen, boisterous self. Caleb had been like that as long as Faith could remember. Faith loved him for it.

A crowd of other shoppers looked at Caleb like he was crazy. They laughed nervously and they whispered into each other's ears. Within a few moments, however, everyone began to notice how talented Caleb was at dancing—graceful, passionate, and agile. Then they continued to shop like Caleb wasn't even there.

As he walked backward, Caleb grabbed both of Faith's hands and invited her to dance with him. As the song "Tutti Frutti" came on, the two held hands while they lifted them up high and put their right feet forward.

"Charleston now!" Caleb shouted.

Music still playing, the lilac skirt of Faith's sundress twirled as she swayed her hips. She looked down at her white, ruffly anklets. In mid-step, Faith fell on her stomach. Gasping, Caleb helped her up to a standing position.

"All right, I think that's enough dancing, Caleb," Mrs. Johnson corrected. Caleb just laughed as his mother shook her head scornfully and went to another part of the store.

"Bye, strange lady I don't know," Caleb joked.

"*I'm* strange?" Mrs. Johnson asked as she raised her eyebrows and pointed at herself.

After they left Bath & Body Works, their plan was to head to Red Robin for dinner. As soon as they were shown to their table, Mrs. Johnson noticed Caleb dancing the Hammer Time behind the waitress. Mrs. Johnson gave Caleb a stern look and said, "I know you're not a show-off, Caleb, but people here don't know that. You already danced at Bath & Body Works—you don't need to do it here."

CHAPTER FIVE

The next day, the auditorium was dimly lit as the teens descended the red-carpeted aisles. Everyone was sitting in their velvety seats. Grace, Faith, Caleb, and Gabe were excited to go to drama club, because Mr. Perry was leading up to announcing the title of the play they would be putting on—although the word was pretty much out. The children waited in anticipation.

"Here is the play we're doing." Mr. Perry pressed his hands together. "We're going to do...*The Miracle Worker*."

"Yay!" Faith and Grace hugged. The friends exchanged fist bumps and high-fives with the boys. There was a cacophony of voices in response.

"What was the next closest vote?"

Mr. Perry paused. "I'm pretty sure it was *The Hunchback of Notre Dame*."

"Bummer!"

"I really wanted to do that one. It's so beautiful."

"Gabe could totally be Quasimodo—he's got a stellar voice."

"Why can't we do a musical?" A bunch of other students concurred.

"I'm a dancer—I wanted to learn some choreography."

"I wanted to sing."

"Maybe you can all look forward to that in our spring musical. But this has been a democratic process," said Mr. Perry. "We have to accept the results. Now, what might lift your spirits, especially you dancers, is that I made a Q&A with the talented and young dancer, Bethany

Xiao, on Saturday. I thought it would be beneficial for you to spend some time with her and learn about sign language."

Exclamations of glee and whispers filled the room as the majority of the kids responded to Mr. Perry's announcement.

"How does she dance if she's deaf?" a student asked.

"Bethany can feel the vibrations of the music in the floor," Mr. Perry stated.

"I know her," Grace whispered to Faith.

"Yeah, me too," Gabe said quietly.

"Grace is obsessed with her." Caleb rolled his eyes.

"I've never heard of her," Faith said, baffled.

"She's a Catholic dancer who dances at events for kids with challenges. She's strong in her faith. She can dance extremely well!" remarked Grace with a grin. "Bethany was named after a village in Jerusalem where Jesus raised Lazarus from the dead."

While Faith listened intently to Grace, she started to feel sick. Seizures made Faith see a bright blue light that made her eyes tired. She closed her eyes even though she knew it wouldn't help. It was still there. The blue light was flashing and slowly moving up and down.

Caleb glanced at Mr. Perry, who was still talking. Caleb, barely audible, remarked, "I've read about her, but never met her. I always wanted to go to one of her conferences."

"You mean the kind where you ask questions and meet her? You can get autographs, right?" Gabe inquired.

"Yeah, but I'd be too nervous. I sent her a letter, but she never replied," Caleb shrugged.

"Why would you be nervous? You're not nervous about anything," Grace commented.

"I'm only nervous in front of famous girls," Caleb replied.

* * *

Warm sunlight shone down on the still-green grass of the Johnsons' front lawn. Sounds of summer were audible: Cars' engines, dogs' barks, and children's calls and laughter. Neighbors took family bike rides, walked their dogs, and jogged past the house. Mr. Johnson was busy mowing the lawn. The front yard smelled like dirt, hose water, and grass. That afternoon, Faith and Grace arrived at Caleb's, as planned. They met Caleb in the foyer of his house. Gabe was coming over with his mother, Mrs. Charles.

"Hey, guys," Faith smiled. "Are you ready to see Bethany at school?"

"I'm freaking out," shouted Grace ecstatically.

"Me, too," Caleb said in a squeak.

"Mr. Perry said we could bring something for Bethany to sign," Faith commented.

"Bethany Xiao...*at our school*." Grace grinned and clenched her fists. "I'm so nervous, guys."

They waited for Mrs. Johnson, who was waiting for her pumpkin bread to finish baking in the oven. She was their ride. Caleb and Faith sat on the island. Caleb got a can of whipped cream out of the stainless steel fridge and sprayed some into his mouth.

"Ew! Caleb!" complained Grace from the couch.

"Let me try that," Faith said. "But hold the end of the can so I can squirt and hold my mouth open simultaneously."

"Sure thing," Caleb said.

"Hey," Gabe said as he walked into the kitchen. He turned to see Caleb holding the can while Faith was squirting. She squirted too much and was coughing. "Eating whipped cream, huh?"

"Yeah, it's my favorite dessert," Faith beamed as she dangled her feet back and forth.

Caleb lay back his head and squirted whipped cream into his mouth.

"I told you! It's not a dessert—it's a topping," Grace called.

* * *

The sun glistened on the windshield as the children drove to school for drama club. Grace was talkative and was excited about meeting Bethany—the total opposite of how Caleb was acting. He was visibly nervous and quiet, which was definitely not him. The weather was still sunny when they arrived in the school parking lot.

After they entered the front wooden brown doors of the auditorium, Caleb froze, hugging his autograph notebook to his chest. After being in the blinding bright light that came from the school hallway, the auditorium appeared dim.

When they entered the auditorium, Mr. Perry greeted, "Hey, kiddos. Meet Bethany."

Bethany had silky, long, black hair. She had a beautiful golden skin tone, perfect lips, and glinting almond-shaped eyes. Bethany was sitting at a table about ten feet away from them.

"Grace and I are gonna go to the vending machines to get water," Gabe told Faith.

Faith expected to see kids crowded around Bethany's table. Apparently, the drama kids decided to get all the sleep they could, since it was Saturday.

"Caleb, what on earth is wrong with you? I've never seen you like this," Faith asked.

"Bethany," Caleb whispered back.

"Her interpreter will be joining us since we can't understand sign language," added Mr. Perry.

"Hey, guys, come over here. Don't be shy," Bethany said through the interpreter. Faith found it fascinating to watch the interpreter signing. Bethany was communicating through sign, and then the interpreter would tell Caleb and Faith what Bethany said.

"Why don't you introduce yourself, Caleb?" Faith urged.

Faith gently led him down the front aisle toward Bethany, who stood up.

"I'm...Caleb," Caleb stammered, his bottom lip quivering.

"I'm Faith and this is my friend Caleb—he's a big fan of yours. He's amazed by your talent and how much you've accomplished at a young age," Faith complimented excitedly.

Caleb simply nodded.

"Thank you," Bethany smiled. She turned to Caleb. "No need to be afraid." She focused on his face and his lips. She was lip-reading. Caleb and Bethany exchanged a clammy handshake. "Do you want me to sign that?" she asked with a welcoming expression on her face. Caleb looked at her. "The notebook?"

Caleb looked down at his notebook.

"Yes, please," Caleb whispered and gave it to her. Bethany turned to her interpreter. The lady mouthed the words that she was interpreting into sign language.

"I love signing autographs for fans.... Hard to believe I have fans. I don't feel famous because I feel ordinary. I'm just doing dancing for fun," Bethany said as she signed the first page with a black Sharpie. "I always loved the smell of a Sharpie." Bethany looked up with a big smile, signing, "There you go! It was lovely to meet you. I'll be answering questions in twenty. Feel free to ask me anything. It was Caleb, right?" Caleb nodded slowly. Bethany turned to Faith. "Would you like an autograph?"

"Yes, please, if it wouldn't trouble you," Faith requested.

"No trouble at all. That's what I'm here for, right? Anyway, I love to see my fans and answer questions—I'm a people person. Who did you bring with you besides Caleb?" Bethany autographed the picture Faith was holding—Grace had given it to her yesterday so she would have something for Bethany to sign. It was a glossy headshot of Bethany. She signed her swirly signature on the light backdrop behind her pictured face.

Caleb walked away to join Gabe and Grace, who had returned from the vending machine.

"Caleb and I brought those kids." Faith pointed to her friends, who were walking toward them. "That's Grace and Gabe. They're cousins. It's a dream come true for my friends Grace and Caleb to meet you. Hopefully, Caleb will ask you some questions."

"Give him some time. How do you know me?" Bethany asked through the interpreter.

"I just heard about you from my friend Grace. I looked you up on the internet last night, and you're a fantastic dancer," laughed Faith.

"Aww! Thank you," smiled Bethany. "I heard you're putting on *The Miracle Worker*."

"Yeah," Faith nodded proudly.

"I can come to one of your practices," Bethany signed.

"Hey, Bethany! I love you so much! I always wanted to attend your conferences or see you perform," Grace rambled as she barged toward Bethany's table.

Gabe, sticking out his hand, greeted, "I'm Gabe, Grace's cousin. It's nice to meet you."

"Your friend, Faith, told me about you and Grace. Nice to meet you, too," Bethany remarked.

Fortunately, the friends got great seats, because the other drama kids arrived later. Grace, Gabe, Caleb, and Faith all settled in their seats at the front of the auditorium to ask questions. A crowd of kids burst through the doors and crowded around Bethany's table. Muggy air filled the auditorium because of the drama kids' breathing and body heat.

"All right, kids. We're going to start the conference now. You can get your autographs later." Mr. Perry held up his hands. He led Bethany to the stage.

"Thanks for having my back when I couldn't talk," Caleb whispered to Faith. "It was so embarrassing."

"You're welcome," smiled Faith.

Mr. Perry gave Bethany a microphone. She handed it to her interpreter with a smile. Bethany's eyes were illuminated by the spotlight that shone down on her.

"Questions?" Mr. Perry asked.

"What genre of dance do you know how to do?" one student asked.

As Bethany signed, the interpreter translated, speaking into the microphone.

Nodding, Bethany replied, "I know how to do lyrical, tap, Irish step dance, jazz, contemporary, ballet, hip hop, and waltz."

"What is your favorite?" another student inquired.

"I love waltz, ballet, and tap," Bethany smiled broadly.

"How long does it take to practice?" Gabe asked.

"My practice starts at 10 a.m. and ends at 6. I dance for eight hours a day since I became a professional dancer. I've got ten classes a week and that's only for jazz, ballet, and contemporary. That's why I'm homeschooled."

"Bethany, my students are putting on *The Miracle Worker* this year. We were intrigued about how people use sign language to communicate," Mr. Perry explained.

"Ah, thank you for contacting me, because I love teaching people. I use sign language to communicate because I don't speak verbally. I started to learn sign when I was very little," Bethany explained. "Does anyone here know sign?"

Grace jabbed Faith in the ribs, whispering sharply, "Faith, you know sign."

"I don't want to be braggy." Faith waved her away.

"Come on," Grace urged.

Faith raised her hand reluctantly.

"You there! Faith?" Bethany pointed to her from the stage.

"I know sign because I started to learn it a few years ago as a second language. I'm homeschooled, too, so my mom let me learn ASL instead of learning French or Spanish."

Bethany signed "excellent" to her. Faith smiled.

"I'm homeschooled because I have epilepsy, and the brain recovers from epileptic activity during sleep," Faith said.

Bethany frowned briefly. "I'm sorry. That's very interesting about the brain, though."

An echo of uncomfortable laughter went through the auditorium.

"I believe people with challenges *still* can do amazing things," Bethany said. "It's more important what you can do than what you can't do."

"Amen to that," shouted a male student.

"Where do you perform?" Grace asked.

Bethany replied, signing, "I dance at charities for small children and teenagers with challenges. The audience pays for tickets to see me, and then I donate that money to a good cause. I'm also hired to dance at theaters for adults."

"Can a person who has deafness learn how to speak?" a pupil asked.

Bethany responded, "Yes, but they can't hear themselves and it takes lots of practice. Helen Keller learned to speak. I once saw a video of her talking, but I'm told it is hard to understand her."

"Do you wear hearing aids?" asked one student.

"I don't have hearing aids, or cochlear implants. Often the Deaf community are reluctant to use cochlear implants or any hearing devices because they don't want to be *fixed*," Bethany continued. After a hesitation, she remarked, "So, *The Miracle Worker*? I love that play, but I mostly enjoy musicals. I can feel the music in my legs and feet from the floor." There was a murmur of excitement in the room as the students took in this information.

"If I did a promposal, would you accept?" another teen boy asked. Everyone, even Bethany, burst into uproarious laughter.

"All right, calm down. Bethany is going to teach you some sign language," Mr. Perry said, crossing his arms.

Bethany spent the next half-hour teaching the basics of sign language, and the kids were disappointed when the time was up and the class ended.

The four friends exited the auditorium. It had rained while they were in the school, and sunlight streamed through the clouds.

"Where was my audacious Caleb?" Faith asked, skipping ahead. She splashed through the puddles.

"I don't know," shrugged Caleb. "My heart's pounding." He placed his hand on his heart.

"You normally take life by the reins," Faith said enthusiastically.

"I know, but when I saw her, I panicked and...I don't know," Caleb remarked, looking down.

"Looks like Caleb has a major crush on this girl." Gabe gently bumped Caleb's shoulder with his.

"Nah," Caleb objected softly, lowering his head.

"Your reaction to your encounter with her says the opposite. You were obviously starstruck," Gabe said.

"It was an awesome experience. Bethany's so nice and outgoing. I love her so much that I want to squeeze the life out of her," squealed Grace.

Faith turned to Caleb, asking, "Do you know her? I mean, not personally, but are you part of the fandom, as it's called?"

"I mean, I've seen her dance," Caleb said. "I think she's gifted."

"You can say that again," laughed Grace.

"I know I won't see her again," Caleb said downheartedly.

Mary and Mark went to Mark's home for dinner, following the same dirt path that Mark had taken that morning.

Mary's mother, who was affectionate and kindhearted, had allowed Mary to dine at Mark's residence that particular evening. It was a rare occurrence, since Mother was markedly assiduous with the daily routine of the domestic household.

Their knees were sore and their throats were clogged from their work. Mark and Mary lugged two bucketsful of water from the stream so Mark's siblings could wash up. Mama had set up a system where she had assigned each child a particular slot of time where they would retrieve water.

As they arrived in front of the farm, many of Mark's siblings stopped carrying their heavy loads of rich earth, or tending to the soil, to gather around Mary and Mark.

"Mark! Mark! You're home," cried his three-year-old sister. Creamy-colored tufts of her hair were hidden underneath her headscarf that flapped in the wind. Little sweaty children in dirt-covered britches and threadbare dresses wrapped their scraped and sunburned arms around the older children's waists.

"Come inside!" a warm, but firm, voice called from the doorway of the creaky old farmhouse. All the children filed into the house and washed themselves. After they had tidied up, the large family sat at the rectangular, antiquated, scratched table. It was in the center of the stone-tiled kitchen.

A fire crackled under a hot pot of broth in a niche carved into the corner of the room.

"Thank you for bringing in that firewood, Mark," said Mama. "That was very helpful."

"You're welcome, Mama," Mark said as he and Mary handed out bowls of broth and pieces of bread.

"I adore your large family," Mary commented.

"Do you fancy you will have a big family akin to ours?" asked one of Mark's little sisters.

"One day, I shall get married, raise children, and live on a farm," Mary began as she sat down at the table with her bread and broth. "Yet it cannot be fulfilled for an awfully long time. I might not get out of the mill until I'm in my early twenties. My whole family relies on the wages I receive. Even though my earnings may be small, I can't leave now, for it's the only money we have to eat. Do you ever think you might get married and have a family of your own after you get out of the mill, Mark?" Mary blushed as she hid a smile at the thought of Mark being married.

"As for marriage, I don't know about the prospect. All I can think about is working to provide for my family," Mark replied, reddening and locking eyes with Mary.

"Your sister Harriet and brother Arthur wrote from the large estate," Mama remarked, picking up a folded piece of stationery paper.

"Why must Harriet live away at that big old house?" asked one nine-year-old freckled sister with waist-length hair and green eyes.

"Because, little Edith, Harriet brings home adequate wages, has good boarding, and has filling meals that I could never offer her here," Mama replied.

Mark scoffed and looked away from his mother, rubbing the stubble on his upper lip. "I know she has clean and good clothes on her back, a roof over her head, and mouth-watering meals. However, she has an overwhelming load of work to do as a scullery maid. She has to wash dishes all day, help the cook, clean the kitchen, empty chamber pots, kindle fires, and wake everybody up at daybreak. Poor Arthur waking up at dawn, cleaning muddy boots, running errands, and emptying all the male servants' chamber pots for sixteen hours."

"Well, everything involves hard work," responded Mama, "especially for people like us. But we just need to rely on the Lord. My ma always quoted Matthew 11:28-30 whenever I was complaining after I returned from the mill. 'Come to me, all you who labor and are burdened, and I will give you rest. Take my yoke upon you and learn from me, for I am meek and humble of heart; and you will find rest for yourselves. For my yoke is easy, and my burden light.'"

"Perhaps Arthur will grow up to be a footman," interjected Edith.

"I always wondered what Mark would look like in one of those fine coats and white gloves," smiled Mary, reddening. "He'd look so handsome and chivalrous."

"I heard from Harriet that they only accept young men who are tall and very handsome. The pick of the crop. They wouldn't accept scrawny, shabby me. Besides, I wouldn't like all the strictures and rigidity at one of those grand houses," Mark smiled.

"I wish I could be one of those fancy little girls who belong to one of those elegant rich ladies, so I could put my hair in those expensive flowers and satin ribbons," said Edith.

"The only reason we let you keep that full head of hair of yours is because you beg us. If your siblings didn't plead your case, I would cut it for practicality and modesty reasons. You must remain humble and not be viewed as vain," Mama said.

"How could you be vain in these circumstances? We can barely eat," muttered an older brother, stirring his broth.

"John! We must always be thankful to the Lord at all times," Mama interjected.

"Indeed, Mama is right," agreed Mark, nodding. "We were busy at the mill today as usual. I do wish we didn't have to work there."

"But you must work there. Mr. Edward has been so kind as to help with our debt on this house and farm. Don't you recall that we owe him money?" asked Mama. "The only reason Mr. Edward's father let me go was because I eloped with your father and afterwards gave birth to Harriet when I was fifteen. I must admit—I don't miss being a spinner—repairing damaged threads."

Edith turned to Mary. "Did your mother work in the textile mills like Mama, Mark, and yourself?"

"Well...my mother was a hired farmhand. She spent most of her days in the heat picking crops and stuffing them in heavy bags. She spent hours hauling large wooden boxes of produce and soil," Mary said.

"You better eat that broth that your sister made for you. She arrived earlier than you at supper to prepare it," ordered Mama to Mark.

"Yes, Mama," answered Mark, nodding.

Mark and Mary washed everyone's dishes and put them away when supper had finished.

"Well, I shall fetch more fresh water from the stream," Mary announced.

"And I will help you," Mark said. He got up while he laid a hand on his lower back. Mary hated to see the effects of the textile mill weaken Mark.

"Will you be all right? I know your back and knees are causing discomfort. I do not like to see you hurting," Mary said softly.

"I assure you," Mark said firmly, "I'm perfectly well. It's all part of the job." Mark shook his head and held up a hand.

"How is your pa?" Mama asked Mary.

"Dad is having difficulty with his knees and back," Mary said. "His knees and elbows are hurting him more as of late. His cough is also worsening—the doctors call it brown lung."

"We will say a prayer for him tonight—won't we, children? Prayer is a powerful thing because Jesus always listens to us—" Mama said.

Edith interrupted and tapped Mary on the arm, saying, "What do you speak of when you go off by yourselves on these little jaunts?"

"We simply discuss what it is to live," Mary responded.

"To live?" Edith looked quizzically at Mary. She hesitated as she bit her bottom lip. Edith followed Mary out the door and took her aside. "Do—do you fancy my brother?"

"You're a very perceptive girl, little Edi." Mary smiled as she laid a gentle hand on her shoulder. Edith beamed up at her. Mary sprinted after Mark.

Together, Mark and Mary set out on the dirt path to the stream, shaded by a verdant-leaved oak.

"I hope we aren't late," said Grace as she pressed her ear to the auditorium's doors. "I already hear people's voices. They sound really good —I wonder who Mr. Perry will pick."

Faith and Grace walked quietly to their seats.

"It's so dark in here," Grace whispered as she motioned for Faith to follow her. The two best friends sat comfily in the front row.

Faith decided to audition for Helen because of her friends' urging. Gathering at each other's houses, they practiced together all week. All four of them were going to audition for a role.

Mr. Perry was watching the auditions. He ordered the behind-the-scenes and lights guy to set the stage. Now, lights were dimmed and the stage spotlights were bright. Seventeen-year-old Tracy stepped confidently onto the stage. Her short, dyed, creamy-white hair was lustrous in the stage light. Her brown eyes expressed determination. She had ebony-colored lashes, and red lips. Tracy didn't smile often and looked serious all the time.

"Of all people, *Tracy*! That snooty girl!" Grace huffed as she laid back in her seat. Gently placing her hand on her forehead, Grace closed her eyes and sighed. With a deep breath, Tracy said her lines. She had great expression and was articulate. Amazingly, she faked a light Irish accent that was perfectly practiced.

"Do you think she has a dialect coach?" Grace whispered and Faith shrugged.

They did the Breakfast Scene and the Water Pump Scene of *The Miracle Worker*. The Breakfast Scene was where the main characters, Annie and Helen, are in the Kellers' dining room. Helen wants her teacher's food, but Annie doesn't let her. It ends up in an exhausting battle. The Pump Scene is where Helen learns language. Her realization that words are connected to things happens as she is pumping water.

Mr. Perry paired everyone up for the Breakfast Scene. Faith was playing Helen at the moment, which was the role she wanted. Grace was Kate Keller, Helen's mother. Caleb was playing Arthur, Helen's father, and Gabe, who was auditioning for Jimmie, followed. Jimmie was Helen's brother.

As part of the scene, Gabe began to fake a dispute with Caleb. After the scene, Mr. Perry said, "Now, kids, you'll have to wait a week until the cast list comes out."

"Aww..." Grace's shoulders slumped.

"I don't know if I'll get the role, guys. I was trying to look serious during the dispute with Gabe, but I lost it," Caleb said as he grabbed a bag of Sour Patch Kids from his backpack.

"I lost it too many times. I kept giggling, and I couldn't keep it together," Faith commented.

A week later, Grace went into her white-painted house, with Faith not too far behind. It was a large house with neatly trimmed, bright green hedges, a brick walkway, bright pink phlox, a dark blue door, and little trees with purple flowers.

Faith proclaimed, "Mrs. Foster! I'm playing Helen and Grace is playing Kate. It's joyous news!"

"Great!" Mrs. Foster said as she kissed Faith and then Grace on the top of their heads. "I think it's going to be a great experience, but a huge time commitment."

Laughing, they went into Grace's room. They began to learn their lines. Faith didn't have any lines to memorize. Because Helen Keller didn't speak, Faith and Grace had to coordinate their movements; it was like choreography. Faith began to help Grace learn the sign language alphabet, which involved making shapes with one's fingers.

"I have to tell Dad that I got the role. I hope he can drive me when I'm at his house on the weekends. I'd hate to miss a practice just because he's too busy at work to drive me."

"Don't worry, Grace, we'd pick you up," Faith reassured.

"He'll want to take me; he's all about theater and stuff," Grace explained. "But he's got so much responsibility at his job. I don't even know if he'll be able to come to opening night."

"How do you even know when opening night will be?" Faith inquired.

"It's already on the school calendar," Grace said.

"Oh, so, that's why I didn't know," Faith said.

"I'll forward it to you in a text. Here, before I forget," Grace said, reaching for her phone.

* * *

After school the next day, the cast began to practice. The set department provided a table, wooden chairs, and dishware. Blinding stage lights shone down on the cast. From backstage, Faith ran to the center of the set to begin the scene.

Tracy, who got the role of Annie Sullivan, sauntered to the table at that same moment. She took her seat. The student who portrayed Viney, the kitchen maid, walked briskly with a dish of eggs. Faith mimicked a blank expression in her brown eyes as she looked ahead. She stared up at the ceiling until she felt her eyesockets. Faith listened to her castmates' lines. Stumbling toward the table, she breathed through her mouth to create guttural noises. Kicking, Faith flailed as she tossed and turned on the floor. Tiring, her voice was dying out from screaming.

Meanwhile, Tracy grimaced as she tasted the cold eggs. She choked them down as she glanced at Faith, feigning disapproval. Whimpering, Faith ran to find her character's mother, stumbling as she rose from the floor. But Faith stopped, her memory fogging over. *What was I about to do?* She began to feel nauseated, headachy, and tingly.

Mr. Perry was right in front of the stage in the center aisle.

"Faith! You were about to run around to find Helen's mother!" he reminded Faith, as he opened his arms wide, holding the script in his left hand.

An uncomfortable moment passed while Faith froze in place, staring.

"Oh, sorry—I'm seizury. I couldn't remember," Faith apologized.

"Oh, brother. We're wasting time," Tracy said.

"Tracy," Mr. Perry said, his voice carrying a warning. "It's okay, Faith, take your time."

Faith went around the wooden square table, resuming her acting. In this scene, Annie repeatedly grabs Helen firmly and places her back into her chair. Resisting, Helen twists and runs away, making growling noises. Near the end of the scene, Annie and Helen are rolling around on the floor.

Finally, Faith ceased her wild dramatics, her heart beating in her throat as both she and Tracy tried to catch their breath. The spotlights' heat beat down on them as they cleaned up the mess and lowered the curtain. Exchanging high-fives, the kids got off the stage, sweating. Faith and the boys were praising each other about their performances.

"You did great," Gabe said with a bright smile.

"Thank you," Faith said as she continued to breathe heavily.

"You're welcome," Gabe said.

"You did awesome," complimented Caleb with a soft smile.

"She did all right," mumbled Tracy, coming up behind them. "I could've done better."

"Playing Helen is hard—I keep hurting myself," Faith smiled.

"Well, you have to be careful," Tracy said grumpily. She soon left the auditorium to go home.

"She's so conceited," said Caleb and lowered his head as he rolled his eyes. "I'm gonna go with Gabe to the vending machine to get a bottle of water and a granola bar."

Faith turned around and saw Bethany, the famous dancer.

"Bethany! You came!" Faith signed and threw her arms around her.

"Yes, I was watching. Mr. Perry sent me an email and invited me to come back here to see you guys practice," Bethany signed. Faith was studying Bethany's signs and concentrating fixedly.

"Can you sign more slowly? It would help me understand it better," Faith requested softly and in sign.

"Bethany!" Grace ran toward her. "Faith and I are going to hang out at my house. Wanna come?" Faith interpreted in sign language for Bethany.

"I don't know. I want to, but my mom would freak out. Mom hasn't met you yet," Bethany explained, and Faith interpreted for Grace. Bethany remarked, "Let me just text my mom and ask."

"I'll text my address to your phone. What's your number?" Grace grinned.

Gabe came back into the auditorium. He walked down the main aisle with Caleb following.

Caleb noticed that Faith and Grace were in a huddle with a silky-haired teen. She looked really familiar!

"Oh, no," Caleb said as he stopped in his tracks.

"What, man?" Gabe asked.

"Bethany," Caleb whispered as he grabbed Gabe's arm and stopped abruptly. Bethany was signing slowly, and Faith was translating.

Bethany turned and saw Caleb.

"Go talk over there, Caleb," Gabe whispered.

"And make a fool out of myself again? I was like..." Caleb nodded with a big, exaggerated smile. "I don't think so, man." Caleb shook his head. "She's so pretty and I couldn't talk the last time. I felt like an idiot."

"Try again—maybe it'll go better this time," Gabe urged. "Come on. Remember when you said you'd never see her again? Come on! This is your chance, man."

"Fine," Caleb said as he walked down the center aisle.

"Where are you two headed?" Gabe asked Faith and Grace.

"My house with Faith and Bethany," Grace replied.

"Nice to see you again," Bethany signed to Caleb. Faith translated for Caleb.

Caleb hesitated and then realized he hadn't said anything. "I mean, nice to see you." Caleb gave a forced, anxious smile.

"You did well on stage."

"Yeah…I mean, thanks," Caleb said.

Bethany turned to Grace. "My mom said I can. She's waiting outside of the auditorium," Bethany explained in sign.

"I should text my mom and say we'll be riding with you. She's probably still home," Grace said as she got her phone out of her purse.

"I'll text my mom, too," Faith said.

"Hey, Mom," Bethany said. "This is Faith and Grace."

"Hi, nice to meet you," Mrs. Xiao said.

Mrs. Xiao was slender, had sleek black hair, and almond-shaped eyes.

"Can you ask the navigator to take us to this address?" Bethany handed her mom her phone.

"Sure, sweetie," Mrs. Xiao said.

"Hi, my name is May. How may I assist you today?" a lady on the line asked.

"Yes, can you take us to…" Mrs. Xiao began. She told her the address.

Once Mrs. Xiao was driving her SUV, Grace streamed "You Are Loved" by Stars Go Dim from her phone.

"Oh, I love this song!" Bethany smiled as she signed.

"Me, too!" Grace giggled. "How do you hear music?"

Bethany set her foot on the car's speaker. "I can feel the different tempos and the bass line from placing my foot on the speaker. I can't hear the words. I can always look up the lyrics on my phone, though."

"That's amazing. I never knew that," Faith said. "Stuff like that has always fascinated me about Deaf Culture."

"I didn't even know people who are deaf could enjoy music," Grace said.

"Oh, yeah, that's one of the common misconceptions about people who are deaf. Did you know Beethoven was deaf?" Bethany asked.

"Cool!" Grace said.

"I believe everyone should hear this song! I love the lyrics because they're deep and meaningful," Faith remarked. "It explains that we don't have to be perfect and that God loves us."

"But Bethany *can't* hear the lyrics," Grace stated.

"No, but reading them while listening helps, and it's enjoyable," Bethany replied.

The girls made a decision that whenever they were together, Faith would serve as a translator for Bethany and for those who didn't know sign. That is, until they learned it.

"I'll be at Dad's music store if you need me. I'll pick you up when you're ready," Mrs. Xiao said.

"Your dad owns a music store?" Grace asked as she slammed the door on the back passenger side.

"Yeah, he named it after me, because we used to dance to his band's live music together when I was super little," Bethany told Faith and Grace. The three of them raced toward the front door of Grace's white house. Warm sunlight streamed through the swaying leaves of a large white oak on the front lawn. Slipping into the house through the front door, the girls laughed as they talked about the play.

"This must be your new friend?" asked Mrs. Foster.

"My friend Bethany," Grace said.

"It's a pleasure to meet you," signed Bethany.

Mrs. Foster looked to Faith, who translated.

"You, too. Make yourself at home," Mrs. Foster said. There was a pause. "What a coincidence! Your friend looks exactly like that Bethany Xiao girl. You know? The dancer you always talk about? You know, the one Caleb has a crush on?" Mrs. Foster commented.

"It *is*, Mom," Grace said as she gave her mom a warning look. Faith blushed as she translated the awkward conversation. Bethany buried her head in her hand and chuckled nervously.

"Oh, sorry. Nice to meet you, Bethany. I'll be doing paperwork in the study if you need me," Mrs. Foster said. She walked silently away. The girls walked down the hall into Grace's room.

Painted gray and pink, Grace's room was spacious and had an oak-finished floor. A sequined pillow that said "Hello Gorgeous!" adorned her bed. On the tabletop of Grace's dresser were bottles of perfume and many lipsticks and mascaras.

"So, what have you been up to?" Grace asked Bethany.

Bethany sat crisscrossed on Grace's trundle bed.

"Schoolwork and dancing, basically. Besides that, nothing," Bethany responded.

Grace was shocked, saying, "Nothing! I thought celebrity life rocked."

"If I'm honest, it's not as luxurious as it's cracked up to be. There are always new dance routines that I have to learn," Bethany sighed, repositioning herself to get comfortable. It took a few moments for Faith to translate.

"How long do you have to practice?" Grace asked.

"Well, as I said, choreography work starts at 10 a.m. and ends at 6, plus two hours of practicing at home. Altogether, ten hours a day. Dancing takes a lot of time, but I love it," Bethany said, signing.

"So, professionalism in dance doesn't come out of thin air?" Faith smiled.

"Yeah, not without hard work," Bethany signed back.

"About the different types of dances: I remember you said something about lyrical? What's lyrical?" Grace asked.

"It's a type of dance that is emotional and deep," Bethany explained. "It's very graceful."

"You mean the type that makes you cry?" Grace inquired with a cock of her head.

"I guess," Bethany nodded. "Do you like to dance, Faith?"

"I dance with my friends. If I must admit, I'm very clumsy. I bump into walls, hurt myself three times a day, and I slip on everything!"

Faith said. "I'm the most ungraceful girl God ever made." They all laughed.

"What are you up to, Faith?" Bethany asked.

"Nothing special."

"I'm busy making costumes after school," Grace said, blowing air through her lips. Flopping on the trundle bed, Grace explained, "I did some research on Deaf individuals. I found a thing called Deaf Gain. What is that?" Grace tilted her head while looking at Bethany inquisitively.

"Deaf Gain means that people who are deaf get something out of their challenge," Bethany explained. "The Deaf World, as it's called, is a close-knit, inclusive community. We gain something from being part of the group—we're supportive, and we share experiences and a language. Deaf with a capital D means that a person identifies as culturally deaf, and a lower case D means someone who is deaf—who can't hear. That person wasn't necessarily raised culturally deaf.

People who are deaf can do amazing things! Some individuals wish to be 'normal' and hide their deafness. Then there're others who love being Deaf. Unlike me, not all people who are deaf know sign or are good at lip reading. There're hearing individuals who think people who are deaf will have a slurred, deaf accent or that deaf people are dull."

"I don't like to be called hearing impaired, because it makes me feel like there's something truly wrong with me. As I said, many of the Deaf community don't like hearing aids and cochlear implants because it makes them feel like they need to be fixed. Speech therapy and hearing devices are very controversial in the Deaf Culture."

"I still don't get how you can hear music," Grace said.

"I can feel deeper tempos or the baseline in my feet or chest. There are times it'll be in my stomach. I also will put my hand on the speaker. I'll dance in my socks, too. When I'm at the dance studio, I'll also use counting and follow the other dancers," Bethany continued. "On the other hand, there are cochlear implants and hearing aids that have

Bluetooth that will stream the music and will adjust the volume according to the person's hearing needs." It took Faith a few moments to translate for Grace.

"Why don't you want those?" Grace asked.

"I prefer not to," replied Bethany.

The girls spent the rest of the evening dancing to Christian music and talking.

Chapter Six

When the sky was pitch black, in the middle of the night, Faith began to seize. Her leg jerked uncontrollably while she groaned; her leg hurt like it had a charley horse. She desperately wanted it to stop. Her eyes lolled as she lost track of time. After what seemed like forever, it stopped. When she became aware, Faith saw her parents in her room, looking concerned.

"That was a bad one," Mom said as Dad kissed his daughter on the forehead.

Sighing and relaxing, Faith ordered her left leg to move, but it was too heavy and was not responding, as if it was paralyzed. After a while, Faith was able to drag her weight-like leg. She gained back the strength to sit up.

The next step after she was able to walk again was going to the bathroom to relieve herself. Mom helped her walk—she was unsteady. This was the first tonic-clonic seizure she had had in the last few months. The rest of the night was filled with nausea sensations. Although she was sick, Faith had a gnawing pain that was similar to that of hunger, but she waited for it to pass. She had a headache, which she always got after a seizure.

* * *

The next afternoon was a sublime summer day. Faith and Grace were practicing one of the first scenes of *The Miracle Worker* at school in the auditorium.

"What is this for?" Faith inquired as Mr. Perry tied a knot in a blindfold around Faith's head.

"You have to learn to be Helen Keller. It would be useful if you had a simulated experience like Helen would have every day. It might help you to navigate around the stage only using touch," Mr. Perry replied.

"Okay," Faith said. "Well, that's weird. As if I'm not clumsy enough already."

"What are you going to do, put earplugs in her ears?" Grace asked sarcastically.

"No, make sounds and correct her if she responds," Mr. Perry explained.

"Anyway, how bad can it be? I always said my eyes were useful, but not dependable due to my hurt brain…. But then again, I barely can see anything in the dark. I was getting my snack last night and I bumped into the wall."

Everyone clapped their hands and called, "Faith!" Faith glanced their way.

"Don't respond." Mr. Perry shook his finger up and down.

Faith stretched out her arms, waving them from side to side. She nearly bumped into a lamp on the coffee table. Faith felt the lampshade and turned the corner. She moved her arms again. Bumping her toes against the table's leg, Faith held one of her Mary Janes and hopped on one foot.

"Let's do one of the first scenes where Aunt Ev, Captain Keller, Baby Mildred, and Kate are in the family room," Mr. Perry said. Faith slipped the black blindfold down onto her neck so she could see. Grace stood and waited from the right side of the stage. Slipping Faith's blindfold back up over her eyes, Grace guided her by her shoulders.

Faith clumsily lowered herself down onto the ground as she crawled on all fours. She lifted her hands and felt a cloth doll that was a prop in the scene, and she tried to act wild and hurried. Faith listened to Grace's soft voice, Caleb's firm one, and Gabe's accented voice.

Gabe has done such a great job with his lines; he sounds like he's Alabamian, Faith thought.

The next scene they did was when Annie and Helen meet.

Between practicing scenes, Faith sat down in one of the auditorium seats beside Tracy as she drank from her water bottle. Grace was talking to Caleb at the corner of the stage, while Gabe was doing his homework on his phone.

"Awesome job," Faith said to Tracy. "I hope I didn't gross you out with my fingers. You know—where Helen feels Annie's face and lips?" Faith laughed.

"Thanks. Do you think you can do the blind thing without the blindfold?" Tracy asked. Faith's brain began to glitch, because she was having a seizure.

"Yeah, I did it when we did The Breakfast Scene," Faith said while she endured a stinging headache. Faith's brain often glitched and seizure pain was usually there, but she was trying to appear happy for her friends.

"Don't close your eyes. You have to keep them open," Tracy barked.

"I know. I can't close my eyes because I have to run in lots of scenes. You can't really see anything when you're looking ahead or at the ceiling anyway." Faith smiled meekly. She clenched her fists as she took deep breaths. Faith blushed as her eyebrows furrowed and her forehead wrinkled. The alarm and confusion were evident on her face. She was trying to be merciful, forgiving, and kind, but she felt uncomfortable that Tracy was yelling at her.

My stomach is sick and my shoulders are tense, Faith thought. She pasted on a strained smile as she laughed uneasily. Tapping her feet, Faith drummed her fingernails on her knees and played with her jewelry.

I'm miserable, Faith thought. She felt the rising frustration in her chest.

Tracy smirked and stalked away. "You're a very talented Annie Sullivan," Faith called after her.

"Back to your marks," Mr. Perry called.

Faith waited for Tracy to begin the scene—the ball was in her court.

I have a horrible headache! It's very tense and sore at the back of my head. I want to throw up! Oh no! Faith thought.

"I'm waiting for you! You need the doll!" Tracy snapped.

"Oh, okay!" Faith said and faked a grin. She was quite startled by Tracy's loudness.

What was I supposed to do? It was at the tip of my tongue. Um... Faith thought. Her mind went blank. She wracked her brain while she pushed through the tightness of her right arm and the tingling of her limbs. The right corner of her lip twitched. Her right eyelid involuntarily moved as her left leg jerked. Faith heard Tracy talking, but it was indecipherable to Faith. She couldn't think at all. She was frustrated as she stood there, frozen and silent. Hearing Tracy say something, she could understand it at the time, but then she immediately forgot what had been said.

"Faith! You have the memory of a four-year-old!" Tracy yelled. Faith was silent.

"Okay, Tracy, dial it back," Mr. Perry said.

Faith said to herself, *Stay calm. It's not your fault that you're seizure sick. Tracy just doesn't understand that. You must treat everyone like you want to be treated and be kind and gentle to everyone. People don't get it; I want my friends to have all the happiness and joys that life and God can give. But...right, stay calm.*

Some seizure symptoms were bearable, but some were intolerable. Tingling and visual disturbances were ignorable, since they didn't bother Faith as much. Headaches, having trouble thinking, nausea, jerking, and tightness were a different story.

Faith sighed deeply as she continued to think good thoughts. *I mean, you want Tracy to be happy and have a good life. I mean, you want what's best for her.*

"Faith?" Tracy asked grumpily. Faith resumed her acting.

* * *

After practice, Faith noticed Bethany was at the side of the stage. It was dark because the curtain was covering up the brightness of the stage lights.

"Bethany's here. Bye, Tracy, boys. Grace and I are gonna head out," Faith said to her friends. Faith, Grace, and Bethany were going to hang out at Bethany's house and then go to a movie.

Faith had a headache that felt like it was pinching her. But she pushed through it. It was just a headache, right? Truthfully, she wanted to go home, but Grace needed her to translate what Bethany was signing.

Faith got her backpack as her dad escorted them out of school. Faith's dad had neat, combed-back, full brown hair, and kind gray eyes. His tragus piercing gave him an artistic look.

Bethany, Grace, and Faith made their way to the parking lot; Dad got into the car and started the engine.

After a time, he pulled into the driveway of Bethany's house. It was a white, pine-green shuttered, quaint house with a picket fence. A small, attractive, lush tree was shading the entrance of the fence. Blue hydrangea and red flowers adorned the flowerbed.

The girls got onto the porch as Bethany unlocked the door.

"I'll come back at six o'clock to drive you girls home," was Dad's concise comment.

"All right. See you then, Mr. Daniel." Grace waved.

"Hey, Mrs. Xiao," Faith greeted as the friends went into Bethany's house. Bethany closed and locked the door.

"Please, take a seat," Bethany said in sign language, gesturing to an upholstered recliner and couch.

Faith sat down in the armchair, and Grace took her seat on the pale blue couch, setting down her backpack. The living room had yellow and light blue themes with wide, glass-paneled windows.

"Hello, Faith," Mrs. Xiao said as Faith continued to feel sick. Grace looked concerned; Faith was dazed.

"What's going on?" Bethany asked in sign language. Mrs. Xiao told Grace what Bethany had asked.

"She's seizing," Grace said in reply, and Mrs. Xiao translated. Grace scooted close to Faith. She turned to her best friend.

Mrs. Xiao asked, "Does it help to sit down for a while?"

"It doesn't help to sit down," Faith said in an annoyed tone, looking up at her. She rested her index finger on her temple. "I'm sorry if I was crabby, Mrs. Xiao."

"No, no, you're okay. I'm crabby when I feel sick. So, I'm trying to understand: There's another kind of seizure besides the convulsing kind?"

"Um...uh...yes," Faith said and wanted to throw up. The room was spinning while her head was killing her. She strained to get the "yes" out. But also, to find the correct answer.

After a few minutes, Faith was able to talk a little more. She said to Mrs. Xiao, "The kind that I'm having right now is called focal aware." Faith stopped talking. "Um...I can't talk right now. Grace?"

"She doesn't lose consciousness, even though she might blank out or have trouble thinking. She might not understand what's being said to her, or she might not remember. For her, medicine doesn't help because she's been on lots of different types of seizure medicine for it. But the one she's on for the convulsing kind helps. That type of seizure is called...I forgot. What is it, Faith?"

"What?" Faith asked.

"What are the convulsing type of seizures called?" Grace asked.

"It's tonic-clonic. I had one of those last night."

"What about lying down?" Bethany inquired.

"Um...that doesn't help either. I think it makes it worse. It always seems to be worse when my body is quiet," explained Faith.

Faith's right arm was tight and pain pulsed through it from seizure.

"It started on the left and it's gone to the right side; that means it's worse," Faith described.

"I think I should call your mom," Mrs. Xiao said.

Faith felt pain in her chest and she felt like she couldn't breathe. The left side of her face was tingly.

"It'll pass—my mom doesn't need to come get me," Faith said. "Let's wait a few minutes."

"Would it help if we turned the lights off, or if you had a drink of water?" Bethany's mother questioned, trying to help.

"Um...um..." Faith said as she wracked her brain.

"What's wrong? You seem in a daze," Bethany asked, concerned.

Faith puzzled for a moment. "Um..." *What was the word?* She began to stutter. "Um...I feel like...uh...foggy."

So sick! Faith groaned in her head. She felt like she was going to cry, but that was only seizure. Usually, she would never actually cry, unless it was really bad. Normally, when she was having a seizure cluster, she was so sick that she couldn't even smile. A seizure cluster meant that she was going through several days of worsened seizures.

"All right, we won't ask you any more questions," Grace reassured and patted Faith's right hand. Her right hand was numb. It was the same feeling that she had when she couldn't lift her leg after she convulsed.

"I'm exhausted from the seizures. I'm so seizury," Faith said. She laid her head back and groaned.

"What does that mean?" Bethany asked.

"Sick from the seizures," Grace explained. "It makes her tired from all that seizure activity going on."

"I feel exhausted like I can't keep my eyes open and I feel like I'm drunk. I mean, what I imagine what drunk might feel like," Faith explained. "I think I have to go home. I'm so sorry, guys." A few minutes later, Faith felt like she had to go to the bathroom. But she knew it was just a sensation. Faith heaved a sigh. "Seizures are so disruptive."

* * *

The following day, warmer than the last, the friends were at Gabe's house. Gabe and Faith were playing air hockey in Gabe's basement. They were cheering each other on. It was a musty atmosphere and, although it was hot outside, the temperature was cool downstairs.

"Ooh!" Gabe cried as he high-fived Faith over the table.

"Excellent," Faith laughed. She wore a long-sleeved, white cotton dress with a pink belt that cinched around her waist. Her bright red hair was pulled back by a thick pink ribbon tied in a big bow.

"Grace's been blabbing on about Tracy," Caleb said to Gabe and Faith as he sprinted down the wooden stairs and entered the basement.

"Don't remind me. I know Grace has been raving on. She's obsessed," Gabe replied.

"I don't feel comfortable talking about Grace when she's not here. Don't obsess over Grace obsessing, guys," Faith said. "Changing the subject here: I found good philosophical questions online."

Caleb groaned.

"We're having our own quality time here. You don't have to join in," Gabe said.

"It's like school." Caleb's shoulders sagged.

"Continue, Faith," Gabe said.

"Okay, like this one: Gabe, what is super useful? Intelligence or wisdom?"

"Wisdom, definitely," Gabe replied.

"Why?" Faith asked.

"You two always ask bizarre questions. Isn't it awkward for you?" Caleb asked as Grace came downstairs.

"No," Gabe and Faith answered in unison nonchalantly.

"I'd rather have life experience and be wise about people and make good life decisions. I wouldn't want to be lacking in wisdom and just be intelligent," Gabe responded.

"Yes, a person could be really intelligent and be horrible, and a terrible decision maker," Faith agreed.

Grace walked over to the black couch and plopped down.

"Why do you need to talk about this? It's not important," Grace commented while she rolled her eyes—curling her legs beside her.

"That's what I was just saying. Who talks about this for fun?" Caleb asked.

"We like talking about it—it really makes you think," Gabe remarked.

"I like sharing my beliefs, feelings, and thoughts," Faith explained to Grace. She turned to Gabe. "Is love something you feel or is it a need?" Faith chuckled.

"Well, God gave us love—it's a huge gift. Babies or life are the greatest gift, too. I mean, the greatest gift God ever gave to women in Scripture is infants," Gabe remarked.

"That's definitely all true. But is love a feeling or a need?" Faith asked.

"I think it's a need," Gabe said and elaborated. "I mean, as humans, we need love since we're social animals and we need friends and affection. God said in Genesis 2:18, 'The LORD God said: It is not good for the man to be alone. I will make a helper suited to him.' When I was little, my imagination was so good at making up imaginary characters. I felt like I didn't need real people. My mom used to tell me, 'Sometimes you need someone with skin on.'"

"I get it—like a real person." Faith nodded. "I'm a big bookworm, and fictional characters seem to be my best friends. So, I definitely know where you're coming from. I get what your mom means—sometimes you just need a real person to talk to."

"The hard part is finding someone," Gabe said. "Okay, back to the love thing: I think love is also a feeling, because you feel it in your chest. But maybe I'm thinking about romantic love. True love has to come with sacrifices. One makes sacrifices for people one loves. Usually, it's a sacrifice of one's time."

"Yes, I agree that love is both a feeling and a need. I believe everyone needs to make sacrifices for their loved ones—so, you're totally right. If you don't make sacrifices for someone you love, maybe you don't love them. Jesus made the biggest sacrifice of all for us through His cruci-fixion. Love is really a choice to will the good of the other, technically."

"Didn't Thomas Aquinas say that?" Gabe asked.

"Yeah, I think so. But I hear Bishop Robert Barron say it all the time," said Faith.

"Love isn't always about the romantic stuff, like dating and Valen-tine's Day," laughed Gabe.

"I definitely agree with that," Faith said.

"Here's another: Is it better to have loved and lost than never to have loved at all?" Faith asked.

"Well, love gives life meaning. I mean, I'd rather love and lose some-one than not love," Gabe smiled.

"Yes, I totally agree, love gives life meaning, joy, and purpose," Faith said.

"You guys are boring. For amusement, I think I'll go lie down and stare at the ceiling," Grace muttered as she went upstairs. Faith and Gabe both laughed.

"Suit yourself. You'll miss out on a lot of deepness going on," Gabe said to his cousin as she walked away.

"Hey, guys, don't mind me. I'm just gonna watch the game," Mr. Charles said as he descended the stairs. Mr. Charles had a dark stubble beard, and curly dark brown hair—the same color as his eyes.

Their cheeks reddening, Faith and Gabe exchanged a glance, as they both agreed nonverbally that their deep talk was over.

"Ooh!" Caleb leaped over the back of the couch and put his arms behind his head.

Faith leaned forward and rested her chest on the back of the couch. She squinted at the TV's flat screen.

"I'm not really into football," Faith mentioned.

"It's awesome, right, Mr. Charles?" laughed Caleb.

"Want to go upstairs in the family room and practice our song for Sunday Mass?" Gabe inquired.

"That'd be nice," Faith said as the friends headed upstairs.

"Come on, Grace, we're going to play songs in the family room," Gabe called to his cousin, who was pouring milk for herself.

The four of them went to the family room. Gabe picked up his acoustic guitar from inside its formal-looking pleather case, put on the strap, and strummed his guitar. The friends sang "Because He Lives" by Matt Maher.

Every weekend, Grace, Faith, Gabe, and Caleb rehearsed a song together at Gabe's house. During the week, they practiced their parts of the song separately. Grace was in front of everyone. Faith was to the left of her best friend. She was slightly back, though. To the other side of Grace was Gabe with his guitar in hand. In the back was Caleb on his stool in front of his drums. He usually left his drums at Gabe's house.

Gabe stopped playing his guitar, and Grace curtsied to the imaginary audience in front of her. Caleb stopped hitting his drums, but his hi-hat and crash symbols still rattled.

"That sounds great, guys!" Grace said. "If I do say so myself." She had her hand to her heart while she laughed. "Gosh, Grace, this isn't a performance—we're praising the Lord," Gabe reminded his cousin. Grace shook her head at him.

"I know that, Gabe." Grace rolled her eyes. "I was just having fun."

"Whatever," Caleb said.

"I'm tentative about singing during Mass in front of the whole congregation," Faith said quietly.

"Don't worry, Faith, you have natural talent," Caleb assured, as he set down his drumsticks.

"Yeah, you sound like an angel," agreed Grace.

"Thank you, but I'm still nervous," Faith said.

"Faith, you just have an audience of One," Gabe said. "Don't worry."

After practicing several times, Caleb reached for his drumsticks, saying, "'Good News' by Mandisa for fun?"

"Sure," Gabe said.

"One, two, three! Hit it!" counted Caleb loudly while he simultaneously tapped his drumsticks together.

Grace walked from side to side and acted like she was singing to everyone in the church. She was really into it.

"Man! We were really selling it!" exclaimed Caleb. "Rocking out, man!"

"Caleb, it's praising the Lord, so it doesn't matter if you're selling it," Faith said. *Oh no! Seizure sick. I was doing okay during...um...during band practice. Why does it come on for no apparent reason?*

"Are you feeling okay?" Gabe asked Faith casually, as Caleb put his drumsticks securely in a pocket that hung behind his drums.

"Good!" replied Faith in a faked, peppy tone. "Everything's fine!"

Gabe scrutinized her face and saw that her eyes looked sad and she looked disengaged.

Stuffing his hands in his cargo pants' pockets, Gabe said, "You look sick. You can tell any of us about how you're really feeling. We like straightforwardness."

"I haven't felt well. It's so frustrating! Right now, I can...um..." Faith's seizure activity increased and started to get more uncomfortable. She had tingling in her legs and feet. They felt numb and her left foot began to briefly twitch. Then, the slight movement went from her left to her right.

"The jerking has gone to your right, which means it's gotten worse, right? It always begins on the left side of your body," Gabe observed as Faith's right foot jerked.

Meanwhile, Caleb tapped his feet to a song he was playing in his head.

"I'll leave you two," Caleb said and jogged out of the room.

"Yeah, I'll be in Uncle Jonathan's den studying," Grace said as she picked up her backpack from the couch.

"I'm so sorry," Gabe sincerely said, looking deeply into Faith's eyes. He gave her an empathetic, understanding look.

Faith's spirit felt better immediately, but, physically, she still felt exhausted and awful.

"Do you want to sit down on the couch for a minute?"

"No thanks, I can stand," Faith declined.

Gabe, you are so understanding, Faith thought. Because of her seizure activity, she had the whole idea, but she couldn't express that thought in words. She stood there in a dazed silence for several minutes. Her frustration began to build until she blurted out, "I'm so sick of this!" She paused. "It's every day now."

"It's gotten worse ever since the summer when I was...uh...thirteen. So sick of it! Like...um...I don't mean to be a drama queen, but it's painful. My head hurts on the right. It's so tight and it throbs."

At that moment, Faith wanted to say more, but couldn't even talk or think. The thought was in her brain, but the speech arrest seemed to come and go.

"My memory's been so bad! I can't even hold a thought for two minutes...um..." Faith's mind went blank. The left corner of her mouth twitched. Her right hand was prickling. It felt like she was being stabbed by needles. Gagging, Faith had the urge to throw up—the sensation rose in her throat. Faith saw clear, crooked, bean-shaped things that were floating across her vision. She followed them with her eyes as they continued to move. Thousands of clear dots, visual snow—"bugs," as she called them when she was little—were blinking, and filled her whole field of vision as they blended in with her surroundings. Even though they were there, the visual snow didn't bother her, because she didn't feel any sensations and they didn't hurt.

A spot on her shoulder was burning and then there was another spot where the pain was piercing through her head. Grasping the wall, she leaned forward unexpectedly. Faith had bad chest pain that made her feel like she was suffocating.

"Oh! Faith, are you all right?" Gabe asked when he saw Faith stumble.

"I have to go home. I'm super disappointed that I have to go so abruptly," Faith apologized.

"It's okay. We can try to hang out tomorrow after school," Gabe reassured her.

Faith went home and rested on the couch for an hour. Feeling well enough to attempt to do some homework on her online program, Faith wrote answers to *Jane Eyre* essay questions. She also had to read current event articles by *World Teen*. During a psychology test, Faith's phone rang, interrupting her concentration.

"Hello?" Faith asked as she picked up. "Grace?"

"I have one question. What were you two talking about after practice?" Grace asked.

"Who?" Faith asked absentmindedly.

"You and Gabe!" Grace said in a high-pitched tone.

"Yes, it was nothing and I was feeling sick at the moment, anyway," replied Faith casually. She tried to brush it off and hoped the subject of their conversation would change. "Your cousin and I are merely close friends."

"*You* are in denial! You like Gabe and you know it. You think he's a fox!" Grace remarked.

"What? What are you even talking about?" Faith asked, confused.

"Oh, my grandma said back in the '70s, when she was a teenager, she used to call hot guys 'foxes!'" Grace explained. She burst out laughing.

Faith chuckled and said, "Fox? Really? Ew! That's weird. Yeah, I do think Gabe is handsome, but—"

"You think he's hot—cute," Grace interjected.

"I don't have a crush on him. Truthfully, his appearance is such a small thing—it has minor importance," Faith said.

"But with me on the other hand, I'm a lovesick teenager," giggled Grace delightedly.

"You are," Faith laughed.

"I like boys," chuckled Grace.

"Wait...what boys? There's Caleb, but he's like our brother. Then there's the male drama club members, but we're not close to them. What boys could you possibly like?" Faith inquired.

"All boys in general," Grace said. The girls cracked up for several moments. "Thanks for lending me that book, *Young Women Only*. It was very interesting," Grace remarked. "Very scientific! Classic Faith that you gave me a Christian *and* scientific book about boys and how they think."

Grace mostly talked about boys and Tracy. It was sometimes hard for Faith to hear about her friend's crushes, because she talked about it for the majority of their conversations. After an hour, Faith glanced at her phone and said, "My mom just texted me and said I have to get off the phone."

"Wow! Already?" Grace asked, surprised.

* * *

The next day, Faith went over to Gabe's house with her friends.

That evening, the gang practiced another song and then settled in for a movie.

Faith needed to sit on the floor because she had to be at a certain angle to see the TV due to her visual impairment. Gabe was transfixed by the film as he methodically put popcorn into his mouth. They ate Cheetos, M&Ms, and popcorn. The boys lounged on the couch and ate contently. Faith sat near Gabe's right foot and Grace sat next to Caleb on the floor as they watched the live-action *Lady and The Tramp*.

"This movie is good," Gabe chewed.

"I agree," Faith concurred as she looked up at Gabe.

"Yeah, dude," Caleb agreed.

After the movie, Grace, Caleb, and Faith danced in the kitchen. Grace emptied the dishwasher while she moved with the music. Gabe was sitting on the island, watching. Music blaring, Grace danced, only using her arms and upper body—her feet stayed on the floor.

A song called "Made New" by Lincoln Brewster came on.

"Dance, Gabe," Grace urged.

"I don't like dancing—I don't love it like Caleb does," Gabe remarked.

"What do you have? Dance-o-phobia? Is that a thing?" Caleb turned to Faith.

"Yes, but it's called chorophobia," Faith explained with a raised finger.

The friends did a conga line and moved their heads from side to side like the lions from *The Lion King*. They put their hands over their heads as they put their right feet out, and then their left. Caleb howled as they linked arms.

"Come on, Gabe, dance!" Faith urged. Taking his hands, Faith danced to the music.

"No, I don't want to." Gabe held up a hand.

Even though Gabe declined her invitation to dance, Faith danced anyway. As she leaned back, Faith put her right foot forward and then the left. Faith spun in a half-circle to the right. Gabe got off the island and stood in front of her. Faltering as she walked a few steps backward, Faith tried to get a foothold.

"I'm awful at dancing," Faith frowned. She stepped on Gabe's foot and moved away. She slipped, and her red-sneakered feet skidded backward and she fell. Faith laughed uneasily as Gabe helped her up.

After they danced, the friends sat in the living room around an ottoman on the floor. Faith knelt in front of it.

"Ooh!" Faith said as she looked down at the little glass candy dish of colorful Skittles.

"Oh! I'm so hungry." Caleb's words were muffled by his left hand as he took handfuls of popcorn, Cheetos, and Skittles and crammed all of them into his mouth at the same time.

"You're disgusting, man," Gabe grimaced.

"Mmm! You guys gotta taste this," Caleb said as he raised his eyebrows. He looked down at the Skittles bowl sideways.

"I wouldn't," Grace said, standing behind the couch.

Shrugging, Faith smiled pleasantly, saying, "Okay."

"You're so brave," Grace began. "I couldn't do that."

Smiling over his right shoulder at Faith, Caleb leaned forward as he squatted, saying, "Dauntless, aren't you?"

"Thank you," Faith said, making a serious, stuck-up face while she straightened her shoulders. She took a handful and popped it into her mouth. She smiled and then grimaced.

"Mmm! Gotta have more. This is really good," Caleb said and crammed his hand in the bowl and mixed all the different ingredients.

"You're so gross, man," Gabe said.

By now, Caleb's lips were purple with streaks of bright orange and blue. "What?" Caleb asked, unaware of the colorful appearance of his lips. Gabe and Faith burst into laughter and fell onto their backs. "What? Why are you laughing?" Caleb inquired.

Grace snorted while simultaneously putting her hand over her mouth.

"I think you've had too much candy!" laughed Grace.

Caleb shrugged. "What's up with them?" Faith just grinned at her dear friend and shrugged slightly. "Wanna watch an episode of *Good Luck Charlie*?" Caleb asked and put a navy-blue bandanna around his head. He sat down with a sigh. Gabe stayed on the floor a little ways in front of the couch. After the episode ended, Mr. Johnson, Faith's mom, and Mrs. Foster came to pick up their children.

*　*　*

On a cold, gloomy afternoon the succeeding day, Tracy and Faith were on stage working on a climactic scene: the Water Pump Scene.

"Break a leg, Trace," Gabe said and grinned.

"Don't call me that, Gabriel," Tracy snapped. Gabe bit his bottom lip as he raised his eyebrows, widened his eyes, and looked away.

"Let's get this scene started," Mr. Perry called.

"Good luck." Caleb jogged up to Tracy, grinning. He gave her a thumbs-up.

"I'm an actress—I don't need luck," Tracy said haughtily.

"Beast!" Grace said through gritted teeth.

As the friends walked out of the school from a side door when practice was over, Faith looked at her reflection that looked distorted in a small, rippling puddle and smiled. Faith was always told she was a hopeful, optimistic person; she could see the beauty in even the most gloomy day. She turned to see Tracy, who slugged the strap of her black duffle over her shoulder. Tracy walked across the parking lot—her boots magnifying her heavy footfall. *I wonder why she always looks miserable?* Tracy looked around the parking lot. The weather seemed to reflect her mood—gloomy and hopeless.

"Faith! Come on! My mom's going to take us to her shop now," Grace called to her best friend as she was climbing into the car. "Bethany's gonna meet up with us. She just texted me to say that she and her dad got there before us."

Exhaust fumed in the parking lot of Mrs. Foster's seamstress shop, as the rain pelted the asphalt.

"Hold still, Faith!" Grace ordered and measured her best friend's waist.

"You already measured everything!" Faith said. She flopped her hands on her legs. She looked at her reflection in the mirror as she stood on a small, round platform.

"I want everything to fit beautifully," Grace said with a perfectionistic's air.

"Things can't always be perfect," Bethany reasoned as she signed. She was sitting in a tapestry upholstered armchair. Faith translated.

"Well, we can try," Grace said and recoiled her measuring tape. "I'm making a beautiful, long-sleeved, mint-green dress with black ribbon trim. Helen's hair's going to be in two braids with matching ribbon tied at the beginning and the ends. I'm so excited that I'm making the costumes for *The Miracle Worker*," Grace said proudly.

"You really *are* good at sewing and clothes-making," Faith complimented.

"Thank you! I try really hard, and I'm being raised by a seamstress," Grace said.

The bells jingled on the door and the girls turned around to see Tracy come into the shop. She marched up to the counter and asked Grace, "Is my costume ready?" She passed Bethany and Faith without acknowledging them.

"No, Tracy," answered Grace and shook her head. "It'll be ready next week for sure."

"How is it *not* ready? What about the blouse and skirt? The bonnet?" Tracy mumbled. She shifted her weight from one foot to the other and looked away.

"No, not yet," Grace said.

"Maybe you're not cut out to be the costume designer!" Tracy blurted and turned away. She slammed the door behind her.

"Oh, boy," Faith said and shook her head in disbelief. Grace buried her head in her hand and groaned. Faith turned to Bethany and translated what had happened into sign language.

"I didn't get the whole thing, but I understood it well enough. Don't listen to her—she's just a brat," Bethany reassured.

"But if she doesn't get along with us, our rehearsals won't go smoothly," Grace said doubtfully.

"True. A house divided cannot stand," Bethany added.

"Excuse me, sorry for interrupting you. But is my suit ready?" Gabe asked as he came in, with Caleb not far behind. "Caleb's as well?"

"Well, yes, Gabe! Let me just get it from the back. Caleb, yours isn't fully finished. It should be done by next Thursday," Grace said and headed for the back room, where she kept the finished costumes she had created.

"Hey, Faith, Bethany, want to come over to my place and play some basketball with us?" Gabe asked. "The rain is supposed to stop in the next hour."

"That sounds immensely fun!" Faith giggled.

"Maybe another time—I've got practice tonight," Bethany declined.

"That's a bummer. Maybe we can catch you another time," Caleb said.

"Here you go, Gabe." Grace handed the hanger over to him. The suit had a transparent plastic garment protector over it.

"So, you like basketball, huh?" Bethany asked Caleb. Faith translated for him.

"Yeah, I really love it. I'm on the basketball team, you know," Caleb remarked.

"That's great," Bethany replied in sign.

"Hey, Grace, want to come over and play basketball, too?"

"No thanks, I'm going to work on homework and the costumes tonight. Anyway, I don't like playing basketball—I only like to watch *other* boys play it. Not you two."

Everyone laughed.

"At five?" Gabe suggested, looking at Faith.

"Sure," Faith agreed. "See you later!" she called while she stood on her toes in the threshold as the boys exited the shop.

CHAPTER SEVEN

Setting down their backpacks on the velvety auditorium seats, the cast began to practice a scene the next day. It was the one where Annie Sullivan is helping Helen pack to go back home. It was supposed to be taking place in the garden house. Students who had made the scenery had set up a shiny, oak rectangular table. Placed on it were porcelain floral dishware and white candles. Encircling the table were matching oak dining chairs, and on the floor was a burgundy Persian rug. On the walls were a simple white wallpaper with little pink roses. There was a china cabinet with several drawers full of fancy-looking silverware and shelves holding silver pitchers. The rest of the set was brightly lit with faux flowers on the sides, and a background of a pale blue sky behind the props.

During a break, Gabe, Grace, Caleb, and Faith were praising each other about their acting.

Tracy was surveying the conversation from afar. She walked over to the group and said, "You need to make your acting more emphatic, Faith. You need to *be* your character and walk in her shoes. Like so!"

She began to act out Helen's parts and then she began to feign a crying fit.

"Nice acting out there," Faith complimented.

"Thank you," Tracy said. She walked away to get her duffle.

"I don't think we'll ever get anything done if Tracy keeps acting like this. I can't stand her arrogance and her putting you down!" Grace said to Faith.

"Oh, just ignore her. It'll work, trust me," Faith said.

Before long, they were practicing the Breakfast Scene again. Tracy had been criticizing the cast all day.

After doing Helen's revelation scene at the pump, Grace took Faith to the side of the stage.

Grace whispered to Faith, "I can't believe Tracy told me how to cry and be in Kate's shoes." They went back to the other cast members. "She thinks, like, she knows everything about acting and directing."

"I think you should struggle more than you do, Faith," Tracy said as Faith finished a scene where Helen is crawling across the floor.

Mr. Perry got up from his seat where he had been reading the script. "Now, Tracy, let me do the directing. Faith can act however she wants to," Mr. Perry told Tracy.

"*Are* you directing? It seems like people are doing whatever they want," Tracy mumbled.

"My job is to guide everyone and give tips—not to completely change how the actors and actresses perform," Mr. Perry responded. "May I have a word with you, Tracy?" When he came back, he said, "Okay, I think that's enough rehearsing for today, kids."

"Whatever," huffed Tracy.

Gabe rubbed his face, the wrinkles of stress showing as he squinted from the bright stage lights.

"Don't worry, everything will be fine by next rehearsal," Mr. Perry promised.

Grace nodded and then caught up to Tracy, who was about to leave the auditorium.

"Tracy, we need to work together to put this production on. If we don't team up, we'll never finish rehearsals successfully," Grace stated.

"Don't lecture me," Tracy replied, monotoned.

As the friends walked out of school and down the pavement, Grace complimented Faith, saying, "You did a great job."

"But I'm so achy in the legs and arms from Tracy trying to get me on the floor for the spoon. Who knew it was hard to crawl under a table in a skirt?" Faith smiled.

"We need to go to your house to meet up with Bethany," Grace remarked.

At precisely 4 p.m., Bethany arrived on Faith's front porch. She knocked on the door and Faith answered.

"Hey, Bethany, how are you? Come in." Faith wrapped her arms around her.

"Thank you for coming to all of our practices," Faith said as they entered the foyer together.

"Oh, you're welcome! It's fun to see how drama practice goes," Bethany signed. She hesitated for a moment. "Gabe's here?"

"How did you know?" Faith asked with a cock of her head.

"I could feel his heavy, thudding footsteps reverberating underneath me," Bethany explained.

"How are you?" Gabe signed and beamed at her as he walked toward the door frame.

"Nice job signing," smiled Bethany approvingly.

"Thanks," Gabe grinned.

"I'm well," smiled Bethany. She let out her wonderful loud laugh. "I was thinking of Helen Keller while I was driving here. Helen was one of my inspirations! We are very similar. I've been told she insisted she could do anything a perfectly capable child could do," Bethany commented. "Like I told you guys before, I believe even if you have a challenge, you can do amazing things. You can be an inspiration, too, if you really try and have a passion for it. Speaking of things you've got a passion for, I hear you guys have formed a band." She clasped Faith's hand. Bethany grinned again, her cheeks becoming rosy. It took Faith several minutes to translate.

"Yeah, we play Christian songs after the closing hymn when the liturgy ends. Today, Monsignor emailed my mom and said he appreciated us singing the closing hymn last Sunday," Gabe said to the group.

"Hey, guys," smiled Grace as she came out of the kitchen.

"I think that's great that you're making costumes for *The Miracle*

Worker. It's so cool! You're a good seamstress—the costumes look awesome," Bethany signed.

Faith translated.

"Maybe I could do a fashion show one day—and then I could donate the money to a good cause," Grace replied.

"Oh no! Not a fashion show. Grace, you did enough of that when you were a kid. I had to sit through a whole program of *you*, showing off your favorite outfits. That's enough. Count me out," Gabe said.

"Okay, you don't have to display any of my future creations," Grace joked as Faith laughed. Grace went into the kitchen.

"Bethany, Caleb's coming over soon," Faith told Bethany in sign language.

"Caleb's a great actor. Keep encouraging him to use his theatrical talents," Bethany said.

"But it's hard to get a job or career in theater," frowned Faith.

"Even though he probably can't get a job in it, Caleb should use it as long as he can," Bethany continued.

"Why?" Faith asked as she cocked her head and put her hands on her hips.

"Because he's talented at it," Bethany answered. "We're all given talents by God."

"Can you believe Tracy?" Grace groaned as she came back into the room and sat down. She was holding a mug of hot cocoa.

"Pray for Tracy; she needs it. God said, 'Love your enemies,'" Bethany reminded, smiling softly.

"She's not *my* enemy," Faith added.

"I'll pray she goes to a different school." Grace rolled her blue eyes. The friends all laughed.

"Good one, Grace," Gabe said.

"He said be nice to them even though they might not reciprocate," Bethany explained.

"I agree—do what Jesus would do," Faith said.

"Don't you get sick of it?" Gabe asked Faith as everyone sat down.

"Trust me. I'm not perfect and saintly. I still get frustrated with her, of course, but I try not to. I know it's not my fault that she's mean. She's probably insecure or something. Truthfully, though, her remarks sometimes bring me down. Still, I try to be nice to her," Faith said calmly, glancing at Grace.

"That reminds me of Matthew 5:43-48. Let me see if I can find it," Bethany signed. She scrolled on her phone for a moment. "Yes! Got it!" She sent everyone the link.

Gabe read slowly, "You have heard that it was said, 'You shall love your neighbor and hate your enemy.' But I say to you, love your enemies, and pray for those who persecute you, that you may be children of your heavenly Father, for He makes His sun rise on the bad and the good, and causes rain to fall on the just and the unjust. For if you love those who love you, what recompense will you have? Do not the tax collectors do the same? And if you greet your brothers only, what is unusual about that? Do not the pagans do the same? So be perfect, just as your heavenly Father is perfect.'"

"How do you do it?" Grace's tone was serious as she stared deeply into Bethany's eyes.

"Pray about it," Bethany signed quickly and patted Grace's hand.

"Easier said than done, Bethany," Gabe said as he scratched the top of his head with his index finger in thought.

"Be nice and polite to her when you see her. Don't expect to have a close friendship with her," Faith advised in a matter-of-fact tone.

"I agree, but be nice like Faith is doing. Include Tracy, exchange friendly words, and try to be reasonable and kind to her. But don't let Tracy walk all over you," Bethany clarified. "I know it'll be hard—it's hard for me.... Just think about it, okay? Can we pray? As it is said in Matthew 18:20—'For where two or three are gathered together in my name, there am I in the midst of them.'"

After Faith translated, Gabe bowed his head, and the four friends crossed themselves.

Bethany prayed, "Please bless Tracy. Bless her with wisdom, happiness, patience, understanding, spirituality, and good sportsmanship. Bless Tracy with a loyal, loving partner, angelic children, and a successful job that she loves. In Jesus' name. Amen." They all crossed themselves and echoed, "Amen."

"How many times do you pray that prayer?" Faith inquired.

"Yeah, it looks like you've memorized it," Gabe added.

"About twice daily for people who need it," replied Bethany simply. "I also pray for all my friends."

"But why do you pray about Tracy finding a job, a husband, and having angelic children?" Gabe laughed. "She doesn't need to get married and have kids quite yet."

"For the future. It's good to pray about that," smiled Bethany, giggling happily.

After waiting for Faith to translate, Bethany asked, "Grace, what do you enjoy doing? I know you like to make clothes. But what else?"

"Crocheting or really any textile art," Grace remarked.

"Hey, guys. I didn't know Bethany was here," Caleb said as he slammed the front door.

"Hi, Caleb," Faith waved.

"I just came from basketball practice. I started learning some new hip hop moves."

"You learned hip hop moves at basketball practice? Segue alert," Gabe said.

"I don't really like hip hop. I'm more of a ballet, tap dance sort of girl. What do you like to do besides dancing and sports?" Bethany asked in sign language.

"Slow down, please. I'm having trouble translating what you're all saying," Faith said, speaking and signing at the same time.

"I like playing the drums, singing, and acting." Caleb jumped over the back of the couch. He landed on the cushions on his back.

"Ah, theater and athletics. You like two *very* different things. Both are pretty cool," commented Bethany.

"Variety is the spice of life." Faith beamed with pleasure and then her left foot jerked. Getting up slowly and looking down at Faith's feet, Gabe asked, "Are you seizing?"

"Yeah," Faith answered as her bottom lip quivered from seizure.

"Below your right eye—it twitched," Caleb said as everyone's faces saddened.

"I'm so sorry you're sick, Faith," Bethany said.

"Thanks. Go ahead, talk." Faith offered them a smile.

"Are you sure?" Gabe asked.

"Oh yeah, go on," Faith replied.

"Let's go to the beach tomorrow," suggested Bethany. "I plan to go with my dad tomorrow afternoon after Mass—bringing friends will make it more fun. The more the merrier."

"Sounds fun!" giggled Grace.

Chapter Eight

Stream water rippled in Mark's sinewy hands as he scooped up water using a bucket, while Mary worked diligently filling another. Mark's lips formed a faint smile.

After a short hesitation, Mark said, "I believe we should leave the mill. It's taking a toll on us to be treated poorly every day."

"What?" The bucket from Mary's hand abruptly dropped and submerged into the water. "I am aware circumstances are grim. But we cannot leave; as you mentioned yourself, our families owe money to the mill owner, and we must stay until we pay in full. You must recall that the mill owner asks for an impossible sum. He would be more than content to keep us in debt forever. Apart from that, when could we depart from the mill? I heard about a boy, Ernest, who was always attempting to escape during lunch hours, and he was dragged up the stairs to the overlooker's loft and put in waist chains before you could even blink! Then he tried to escape the loft only to be callously beaten senseless...."

Mary bit on her bottom lip nervously and looked down at her leather boots. "We might leave of our own free will someday, but we can't escape."

"Naturally, we would leave in the dead of night," said Mark.

"Leave our families when they need us so?" Mary inquired, her dark brows furrowing.

"My mother always says we could stay at my uncle's in the case of calamity," Mark reassured her. "I could get a safer job, and we could purchase our own land. Our families could reside with us."

"I suppose so..." Mary's voice trailed off.

"We could board a locomotive," Mark suggested.

"Perhaps," sighed Mary. "I shall go home presently. I will meet you once again tomorrow?" She raised her eyebrows.

"Yes," nodded Mark. "Mary..."

"Yes?" Mary turned around as Mark looked at her with a deep seriousness.

"Contemplate leaving, won't you?" asked Mark.

"I shall," Mary said, biting her thumbnail.

Once home, Mark collapsed onto his bed to hear the whistle blow in what seemed only to be a few minutes. Mark opened his left eye to see that the rising sun was streaming through his bedroom window. Mark looked down at himself to see that he had slept in his clothing.

Time to start the whole schedule over again.

Sunday was clear and windy. The five friends headed to the beach in Mr. Xiao's black van. It was crowded with the five of them all sitting together. The children sang Christian music on the way.

"We should totally get a paddleboard," Caleb said. "I'll be like 'whoo!'" He shot his arms into the air, narrowly missing Grace's head.

"But, Caleb, you'd have to learn first. You can't just jump on and miraculously know how, and be good at it," Gabe reasoned.

"I'm sure I'd be good at it," said Caleb. "I could win a championship! Too bad they don't do it at the Olympics yet. I could win a gold medal."

"I'd settle for a Jimmy Award," Gabe mumbled. "How much do paddleboards cost anyway?"

"Let me search it up," Caleb said, reaching for his phone. "Ooh! Big range of prices."

Faith joined in the laughter. Windows lowered, hair blowing, the three girls were smiling.

"I'm going to the launch site to kayak now, kids," Mr. Xiao said as he took his kayak off the top of the black van. He stroked his dark beard, got his baseball cap out of the car, and put it on his head. He had slick black hair, and dark brown eyes. "I'll have my phone, so give me a call if you need me."

"Do you need help with that, Mr. Xiao?" asked Gabe.

"No, I've got it, buddy," Mr. Xiao said as he lugged his orange kayak down to the beach.

The kids headed to the metal stairs that led down to the shoreline.

Caleb yanked Gabe forward and soon they were roughhousing in the water and enjoying themselves.

Grace rolled her eyes at Faith's clothes, and, upon discovering that Grace was upset, Faith came over.

"Faith, you *really* couldn't find any other outfit more appropriate for the beach?" Grace sighed. "I'm going to the restrooms. Be right back." She pointed toward a pine-green-colored building.

Caleb sprinted back toward Faith, and he told her, "Bethany and I are gonna run to the car and get the picnic basket and the blanket." He tapped Bethany on the shoulder, and they made their way toward the parking lot.

"It's kind of cool. Even though Caleb doesn't know sign very well, he and Bethany can still bond over dancing," Gabe commented as they watched Bethany and Caleb dancing together in the parking lot.

"Yeah, it's really sweet," Faith said.

"Do you want to go down by the water, Faith?" Gabe asked, pointing to the lake with his thumb, his creamy-colored hair blowing in the wind.

"Gabe and I will be near the shoreline," Faith called over her shoulder to Bethany and Caleb, who were approaching them.

Gabe sprinted back to Faith and helped her down the rusty staircase. They ran toward the foamy water.

"You know what, Gabe? Surprisingly, I'm more comfortable with boys, because they're less dramatic and more easygoing. They do jump and run a lot, though," Faith began, and Gabe laughed. "Girls scream a lot and it rings in my ears. I figure it'd be weird at this age if I wandered toward the boys, though. I believe not all boys are rude and immature."

That was weird, Faith, Faith thought as she looked down at the sand.

Gabe was smiling and nodding. He looked down at the soft sand, which fell away as their bare feet made impressions.

"I did some further research on the Deaf Culture. It's so amazing!"

Faith said. She stepped on a twig. Then, she hopped on one foot as she looked at her heel to see if it broke the skin. Gabe picked up a flat rock and tossed it up and down in his palm.

"I know—I've also been studying about it in my free time," Gabe nodded. "I like studying about different cultures."

"Me, too. It's really cool that the Deaf have their own linguistic culture," Faith nodded. She looked down at her gray jumper and black tie, and adjusted her black newsboy cap. Her black vest rustled.

"I love that you're not afraid to wear stuff like that," Gabe said, looking at her outfit. "...even to the beach." They burst out laughing.

"I love what I'm wearing. I don't care what others think. Don't we all do stuff that we love that others would think was not in or trendy? I think you should do what you love.... I act boyish, feminine, mature, and then juvenile."

"I guess that shows you have a lot of confidence," Gabe chuckled.

"I strongly believe: Be what God made you to be. He loves His creations and He doesn't make mistakes."

Gabe took in the meaning of her spontaneous disclosure.

"That was some speech there. I liked it," Gabe grinned.

"Thank you," Faith said.

"I really like having deep conversations with you, Faith," Gabe said.

"I enjoy having them with you, too, Gabe—communication fascinates me."

Gabe remarked casually, "Yeah, I mean, you learn so much through communication. Honesty is very important, too. If you don't have trust and honesty, it all tumbles down, you know? Communication, trust, and honesty are the fundamentals of a relationship."

"You have to have all three—communication without honesty isn't any good, and you can't have any trust without honest communication," Faith agreed.

"It's amazing because feelings, beliefs, and thoughts are shared. And I agree with you, Faith, about differences. Weirdness and differences show courage—individuality! We're unique because God made us that way. We're like God's snowflakes, but with a longer lifespan and personalities."

Faith smiled.

"That was so awkward!" Gabe reddened.

"I can't wrap my mind around how He made all the people in the world—people who've existed before us, and all the people to come—unique. There'll never be another you and another me exactly like us. Each life is precious."

"If we don't have life, we don't have God's creations and don't have anything. It's amazing what God can do through the love of a couple," Gabe commented.

"Yeah, in only nine months! It's crazy!" Faith laughed.

"I've noticed a lot of girls don't want to talk about profound subjects," Gabe stated.

"I don't care what we talk about. When a boy dates me, he'll have to talk about all kinds of deep stuff!" Faith leaned toward him as she opened her arms wide and looked up at the fluffy clouds in the sky. "You have to take the crazy with the Faith."

Taking out his phone and showing it to Faith, Gabe remarked, "On that same note of talking about babies—look at this. My photo app brought up a photo from fifteen years ago. This is Mom at the hospital with Dad and Zach. I'm on her lap."

In the photo, nineteen-year-old Mrs. Charles was wearing a teal hospital gown and was covered in heavy, coarse blankets. Mr. Charles and Zach leaned over the bed's bars. Baby Gabe, with his mild blue eyes, was cradled in his mother's arms. Mrs. Charles' honey-colored hair was dampened with sweat.

"You were so soft and fair-skinned," Faith smiled. "You were a cute baby."

"No, I wasn't," Gabe chuckled.

"Your mom grew up on a horse farm with your Aunt Kim, and their parents, right?"

"Yeah," nodded Gabe.

"What was your mom like at that age?" Faith inquired.

"Mom was a very quiet girl who enjoyed the Bible and tea. You love hot tea, too, right? You're an old soul, Faith," Gabe smiled at her. "Did you know my mom actually knew my dad since they were thirteen? Dad had been helping out as a handyman alongside his dad on the farm."

"What was your dad like as a teen?" Faith asked.

"Well, I only know from pictures and old videos, and what my family tells me. Very awkward, you know—lots of shaving nicks, acne, and he had oily skin. He used to always wear these terrible baggy overalls and this wrinkly shirt. One strap was always unbuckled. Dad also had braces."

"So not at his best as a teen?" Faith asked.

"See this guy here? This is my bio dad, Zach." He pointed to the curly-haired young man in the picture who was wearing a bandana on his head.

"Oh yeah, I see. I always think of Mr. Charles being your biological dad," smiled Faith.

"Me, too, sometimes. Zach was this dude who had this old red T-Bird, and he was charming. He used to help with the horses, too. Zach only stayed for a few months after I was born, and then we never saw him again. Dad treated me like his own and helped support my mom and me. He had always loved my mom, but was too shy to tell her. Finally, Dad proposed to my mom at my third birthday party—it was a *Go Diego, Go* party, in case you were wondering." He and Faith laughed together. "Obviously, she said yes." He cracked up. "So I call him Dad. He is my dad, and he's the only dad I've ever known."

"I'm so glad that your mom chose life," Faith said.

They ascended the rusty stairs and sat on a grassy flat elevation overlooking the beach. Faith lay flat on her back and exhaled. Gentle rays of the bright sun seemingly reached out to touch Gabe and Faith. Now that the wind had died down, it was a warm day and everything was tranquil.

"It's really beautiful outside," Gabe observed.

"Yeah," Faith whispered.

"They say this will be the last nice day before the harsh autumn," Gabe exhaled and put his arms under his head.

"God's handiwork," Faith smiled.

"You can say that again," Gabe said.

"I'm glad we've formed a band where we can play music to praise Him. Have you ever thought of writing Christian songs?" Faith inquired.

"If I ever became a songwriter, I'd become a classical music composer, a Christian contemporary artist, or a Broadway composer. I can't decide," Gabe said. "You sing really beautifully. Have you ever thought of having a career in it?"

"No, but thank you! I like that you play the guitar—that's cool. You're really talented at it. What are you learning on the guitar right now?" Faith deflected.

"I'm learning my favorite song: 'Free' by Riley Clemmons," Gabe answered.

"That's a good one. My favorite is 'You Are Loved' by Stars Go Dim," responded Faith. "Gabe, do you like singing more than the guitar?"

"I love to sing. Well...I don't like solos. It's interesting, because I'm not as nervous when I've got a whole choir singing with me," Gabe said. Faith chuckled. "So, I probably like singing more than playing the guitar."

"So, you don't want to be in the spotlight," Faith clarified.

"Yeah, you get it," nodded Gabe, smiling.

I like how he carries himself confidently. Other people wouldn't be able to tell that he is shy. She smiled brightly at Gabe, her dimples showing. Eyes shining contently, she said, "Wow! The way the sun is glinting off the lake is stunning!" Faith pointed to the lake.

He's so handsome, and his smile is charming. Gabe has captivating, shimmering eyes—very expressive, gutsy, kind, and joyful. He's always ready for an adventure. He has a contagious laugh that is almost as infectious as his smile—his lips are so kissable, Faith thought. *He's so kind to me. Wait! No! He's your best friend's cousin! But he's so gentle and amazing! So talented...stop it! Gabe makes me burst with joy and he's cute! Does he like me? I mean, the way he glances at me sometimes? No! He's just being the sweet guy he is. Surely you're misreading his facial expressions.*

Faith turned around to see Grace approaching them. Caleb and Bethany were following her. "All right, we're back. Sorry we were gone so long. We surprisingly met up with one of the boys from drama in the parking lot," Grace said as she carried a heavy basket by her side.

"Who?" Faith asked.

"Ethan," replied Grace. "This is super heavy. It's a killer."

"Here's another bout of Grace's drama," Caleb exhaled.

Gabe elbowed him, saying, "Caleb, that's not nice."

"Can I help with anything? I feel kind of superfluous," Faith said.

"What is this, the SATs?" joked Caleb, scoffing. The friends laughed for a few seconds.

"Are you sure it won't be too *laborious* for you?" Gabe asked jokingly. "Do you want me to carry it?"

"Would you?" Grace asked, hopefully.

"She can carry it herself, dude," Caleb said. He had a blanket under his arm. He carried another basket of drinks and snacks. "What's with all this difficult vocabulary?"

"What's in here, anyway?" Bethany asked in sign language. Faith translated.

"Oh, sandwiches," Grace said.

"I've got the napkins and plates," Caleb said, his black bangs fluttering against his forehead. He looked down at the heavy basket gripped in his right hand. "Chips, Cheetos, and good junk stuff like that. Gabe, can you go back and get the cooler? I've got pop and water in there," Caleb said as Gabe went to the van. "Let's do this! I'm so hungry I could salivate. I already am," Caleb laughed. "That's my SAT word for the day."

"Like that's an SAT word. I knew that word when I was two," Grace said.

"Probably because the pediatrician diagnosed you with excessive salivation," Caleb laughed.

"He did not!" retorted Grace.

Gabe set down the cooler and the snacks.

"I wish we had an umbrella," Grace said.

"It's okay. It's refreshing to feel the nice weather," remarked Faith. She wore a bright smile.

Bethany began to hand out the chip flavors to the people who wanted them. Faith gave more napkins to her friends.

"You can never have enough napkins," she joked. Everyone laughed.

"We should pray," Grace said.

The friends folded their hands and made the Sign of the Cross. "Bless us, O Lord, and these Thy gifts which we are about to receive, from Thy bounty, through Christ Our Lord, Amen." They made the Sign of the Cross again.

"What is your favorite parable or Scripture?" Bethany asked in sign, as everyone settled in to eat. Faith translated.

"I love when Jesus walks on the water. I even made a drawing of Him when I was little," Caleb remarked.

Bethany tossed her head back and laughed a soft laugh.

"I like the Road to Emmaus—I always wish I could've been there so Jesus could teach me about what all the Scriptures mean," Bethany signed.

"I love that one!" Faith agreed. "I like when Jesus feeds the 5,000."

"That's a good one." Gabe nodded. "The multiplication of the loaves and fishes."

"I like the Scripture when the two men on the roof lower their friend with special needs on the mat," Grace said. The friends nodded in agreement.

"I love when Mary Magdalene meets Jesus after the Resurrection," Gabe said.

"The best one yet. That's the story that makes us Christians," Bethany signed.

A pause ensued.

"How did you strengthen your faith, Bethany?" Gabe asked.

"I strengthened my faith mostly by listening to Christian music, reading Christian books, and memorizing Scripture." A smile flickered on Bethany's face.

"When did you start dancing, Bethany?" Caleb asked.

"When I was five years old," Bethany answered in sign.

"What drove you to become a professional dancer?" inquired Caleb.

"I don't know, but I knew I had a passion for dance. My mom's friend taught me how. I wanted to spend as long as I could doing what I love. What I mean by that is—I know someday I'll get older, and my body won't be able to dance," Bethany smiled. Everyone nodded in agreement and sat in silence.

"I like your shirt," Faith said and gestured toward Caleb's bright blue shirt that said "Kindness Is Always Cool."

"I believe we should be kind to everyone because we never know what someone's going through. Kindness is always cool, like your shirt says," Bethany signed as she shielded her eyes from the sun.

They passed the time by talking and walking on the beach. The afternoon seemed to fade as quickly as it had begun.

"Wow! It's getting kind of chilly," Caleb began. "Want to go home and play some basketball in the driveway, Bethany?" Faith translated.

Bethany nodded. "I should probably text my dad. I imagine he's done kayaking. Ready to go?" Bethany asked as she and Faith linked arms.

"All set," Gabe said.

"This was such a fun day," Grace remarked.

"Let's load into the van," Caleb said.

Chapter Nine

At drama practice the next afternoon, Tracy and Gabe did a scene together. In this scene, Annie Sullivan has a nightmare, and then Jimmie Keller discourages her by saying that she doesn't have the ability to help Helen.

"Good job!" Gabe said to Tracy as he sat down on the edge of the stage.

"Thanks," Tracy said with an air of disinterest and walked away.

"That evil girl!" Grace whispered. Faith and Grace were on the side of the stage.

"Don't say things like that," Faith whispered.

"But it's true," protested Grace.

"We don't know her motives," Faith said as she saw Tracy approaching them to get her duffle. "My friends and I had a picnic on the beach, Tracy. It was nice and simple. Maybe next time you'd like to join in?"

Tracy stared at her blankly.

Faith continued, regardless. "Do you like going on picnics?" Grace jabbed her in the side and Faith winced, but kept her face peaceful.

"No. As if I would like to join one of *your* picnics," insulted Tracy. Grace clenched her fists and Faith laid a gentle hand on her arm.

"Okay, well, have a good day, Tracy. I thought you did excellently," Faith said. All of her friends noticed her calm, warm, friendly expression.

At the side of the stage, Faith sat down and put her hat on her head. Gabe strode over toward Faith, but Tracy grasped his arm.

"Why do you think she dresses like that?" Tracy asked Gabe, furrowing her eyebrows as she indicated Faith, who was wearing her white crinoline hat. It matched her white, dotted Swiss dress. She held her white Mary Janes by the heels."Those loopy braids," Tracy said. "All that *perfect* lace? Come on! Everything she wears has so much flowery stuff. The big bows, the high ponytails? What is she—like a three-year-old? Why would you wear stuff like that?"

"Faith is trying to be your friend. She didn't do anything to hurt you," Gabe said in a calm tone. He was steadfast.

For a moment, Gabe looked angry and upset, but then he returned to the same calm expression. Faith remained at a distance. She was talking to Grace at the other side of the stage.

"Positivity. That's Faith. Personally, I think her joyful mood is kind of contagious. Tracy, have you ever noticed how kind she is to *everyone*? How aware of everyone and everything?" Gabe asked. "Again, she hasn't done anything to hurt you. Why don't you leave her alone?"

"I should go," retorted Tracy. She made brief eye contact with Gabe as she crossed her arms.

"Why did you treat Tracy so nicely?" Grace asked, her eyes glaring into Faith's eyes.

"What good would it do if I treated her like she's treated us?" Faith said composedly.

"But doesn't she make you go nuts?" Grace asked emphatically.

"I wouldn't say nuts, but she does bother me at times. But I don't want to show it. I don't want her to get angry just so I can feel the victory of upsetting her. I also don't expect any kindness back," Faith explained, shaking her head. "What are you going to do today?" Faith asked, changing the subject.

"Well, I'm gonna touch up those *Miracle Worker* costumes after homework." Caleb approached them. "Caleb, you got anything special?" Grace asked over her shoulder.

"Nah, just boring old homework," Caleb responded.

Faith watched Tracy pack her things away in her duffle and noted that Tracy's colorful red lips and flawless skin were ravishing. Yet, she never wore a smile. Her brown eyes were miserable. Tracy looked so... so solemn. Her eyes—they were magnificent; a beautiful dark brown, bright and wide. They were really on guard, though, as if someone was hurting her, and she was shielding herself so she wouldn't get wounded. Tracy's eyes were drenched in sadness with a tinge of tragedy. Although she had a callous demeanor, her jaw was tense with worry.

Faith watched Tracy walk away and noted she put more weight into every step she took.

* * *

During the afternoon, when the sky had puffy white clouds like in a picture book, Faith's phone rang on her lavender, floral-painted table in her room. She picked it up and saw that it was Gabe.

"Hey, Faith, how's it going?" Gabe asked.

"Pretty good, and you?" smiled Faith.

"How was last night? Did you sleep well?" Gabe continued.

"Not so well. Did you hear from the other guys?" replied Faith.

"I haven't heard from any of them yet, but I just got home from choir practice," Gabe responded.

"Grace and I usually talk to each other every day. We FaceTime mostly," Faith explained. "What are you singing in choir?"

"We're singing 'Reckless Love' by Cory Asbury, 'Remind Me That You're Here' by Jason Gray, and 'Hills and Valleys' by Tauren Wells," Gabe answered.

"Wow! I love those songs! They're so beautiful!" A long hesitation ensued. "I don't feel so special right now," Faith admitted. "Um... um..." Her wrist jerked. "Um...my head hurts. I wish my seizures could go away."

"I'm very sorry. Maybe it will go away soon. We can hold onto hope," Gabe commented. "How is your math coming along? Do you want to talk? You don't have to answer, because I know you can't think well when you're sick with seizures."

"They ebb and flow sometimes, as you know. I know how math works and I memorize the formulas...uh...and equations for a while. Subtraction is the hardest, believe it or not .... The next day after I practice math, I get rusty, but, in three days, what I learned is totally gone. Mom just says to do math every day.... Um...create a habit of doing it every day, and you'll never forget," Faith remarked.

"Are you feeling better?" Gabe asked.

"A little, but it will only be momentary," Faith said.

"How is your memory? Has it gotten worse?" Gabe asked.

"My neurologist says my frequent seizure activity has made my memory worse. Here's an example: normally, Mom and Dad give me a task to do downstairs and when I get there, I forget and I ask again." Faith started to get confused.

"That's horrible," Gabe said. "I'd hate to have trouble with my working memory. I learned about memory in my school's neuroscience class."

"Actually, I'm confused right now. Hang on, Gabe. Give me a sec...." Faith paused for a moment. "I'm always sick and in pain, and so I can't think. It's not fun. I *can* have fun, but not as much fun as I could have if I weren't sick," Faith said.

"I know—it's terrible," Gabe said, his voice full of compassion.

"I can't sleep because of the pain. Last night, I got to bed around nine-thirty. On a good night, I fall asleep at eleven or twelve. On a bad night, I fall asleep at two or three in the morning,"

"Mmm-hmm. I don't like that you have insomnia because of seizures," Gabe said.

"Yeah, insomnia isn't fun," Faith said as she chuckled uneasily. "I watched an episode about the science of um...give me a minute...nonverbal communication. It's a college course. I had a hard time paying attention because I was confused because of my glitchy brain. Um...I can't think...I have a headache. Um...Sometimes sarcasm helps, like, saying, 'epilepsy is great' or 'it helps everything.' Sometimes humor helps. Ow, my headache is really bad. Gabe...oh my right foot is zizzy and I have chest pain." She hesitated and sighed. "Anyway, your birthday is coming up."

Faith began to feel better, but every time a seizure finished, another one started and she grew more tired.

"I have to call you back, Gabe. I'm too sick," Faith said.

"Yeah, we can try again in an hour. How does that sound?" Gabe asked. "I was enjoying talking to you, Faith."

"I was having a good time talking to you, too, Gabe. I feel disappointed that we have to end our conversation," Faith said.

Faith called Gabe after an hour of resting. She attempted schoolwork, but it wasn't working out because she couldn't think straight or remember what she had learned. She was very disappointed and frustrated that she couldn't study.

"Hey," Faith said.

"Hi, Faith, are you feeling better?" Gabe asked.

"Yes, I feel a lot better," Faith said.

"I was just doing homework," Gabe said. "On the subject of my birthday that we were talking about earlier: I can't believe I'm going to be sixteen. But, Faith, your birthday is in December," marveled Gabe. "And you're going to be sixteen, too."

"I know! I can't wait! I'm super excited," laughed Faith. "When is your party?"

"I don't know yet. Mom and Dad are thinking on the actual day," Gabe replied. "I already have a list. There's, like, only four things on there. It's mostly...like, ideas."

"Great! Can you send it over?" requested Faith.

"Sure, I'll send it in a text tomorrow," Gabe responded.

Smiling, Faith exclaimed, "Fantastic!"

"Did you finish your schoolwork?" Gabe inquired casually.

Faith replied, "Yeah, took a longer time than I thought because my memory and train of thought weren't working right, but I finished it. I just need to finish this segment of math. It's just my last page of it."

"What is it?" Gabe asked.

"Algebra. It's actually fun," chuckled Faith. "But my favorite subject is language arts—like vocab, reading, and writing. I like challenging books from the Victorian and Edwardian times, because I like the archaic words."

"That's the Faith I know," Gabe said. There was a short silence. "Well, I should let you go. I gotta do a little more school, and then I'm gonna practice my piano and guitar for a while."

"All right, it was nice talking to you," Faith said. "Don't forget to send me your list!"

"Nice talking to you, too, Faith. Oh, yeah, I will totally shoot that text to you. All right, bye," was the reply.

"Yeah, cool, thanks, bye. See you soon!" Faith said. After a pause, they both hung up.

Following her homework, Faith's phone was indicating a text.

Faith saw Bethany's name on the screen. She picked up her phone.

Bethany: Hey, Faith. How are you? I just finished up studying.

Faith: Me, too.

Bethany: What have you been doing?

Faith: A while ago, I was talking to Gabe. His birthday's coming up.

Bethany: How old is he going to be?

Faith: Sixteen!

Bethany: Wow! That's old! Ha, ha! Tell him congrats for me.

Faith: I will.

Bethany: I noticed while we were at the beach that you and Gabe went off by yourselves. You two sure hang out a lot. Gabe always talks about you. He seems fond of you. Do you like him?

Should I tell her? I didn't think anybody knew it. Yeah... I should. We're good friends and she's awesome, Faith thought to herself.

Faith: Yes, he's very sweet and kind.

Bethany: I like him, too, but not romantically.

Faith: Ha, ha! I love you so much!

Bethany: I love you, too! Here are some Christian songs. Let's share songs.

Faith: That sounds lovely.

Bethany: Terrific!

* * *

Faith was talking with her friends at drama practice. It was hard to act. She was flustered, because she had a burning and tingly sensation in her forehead. It was like electricity, which she called zizziness. A seizure began on the left side of her body and moved to her right, which she felt as a tight leg. Her arms were jerking and she had twitching eyelids.

"Everyone—take twenty." Mr. Perry smiled sympathetically at Faith. He went over to her. "Is there anything I can do? Do you need to take some meds, or do you need to take a break?"

"Thanks for asking. I just took my meds a little bit ago. They should kick in soon. No, nothing you can do," Faith replied.

After twenty minutes, Mr. Perry ended the break and called the group together. "Let's end practice for today, and try again tomorrow."

* * *

"All right, action!" Mr. Perry said. They were doing the scene where Kate and Arthur realize that they need to find a solution for Helen, who's frustrated and really wants to communicate. Helen, in a rage, throws papers on the floor from Arthur's desk.

Picking up the papers with Gabe and Grace, Caleb—breaking character—complained, "My back is killing me from picking up these prop papers from the floor and putting them back on the desk."

"Oh, come on, guys! At least we rocked this time," Faith optimistically said.

Mr. Perry interjected, saying, "Okay, kids, let's get back into acting."

At the end of the scene, Helen falls on the floor in a tantrum. Frustrated that she can't talk like her mother is doing, Helen slaps her mother's face. Kate ends up weeping.

"I can't believe you guys cried on cue," Gabe said to Faith and Grace.

"Yeah, it's fun to cry on cue," chuckled Grace.

"I agree. The fall in this scene isn't as bad as the ones in the eating scenes," Faith said with her hands on her hips. "It was pretty hard to whimper and make that sound in my throat for a cry. I have to be careful playing Helen. I might injure myself or ruin my voice."

Grace turned to Gabe. "You're good at playing Jimmie, because you play him accurately. I mean—the way he's so obnoxious and your accent is spot on!" She turned to her girlfriend. "Faith, the slap was really realistic. It was firm, but didn't hurt at all."

The next scene, which they worked on four times, was the Sewing and Letter Scene. In this scene, Annie continues to teach Helen in her bedroom.

Later, Tracy and Faith did the Doll Scene, where Annie teaches Helen her first word, and her teacher begins to see how difficult Helen is. Faith got the giggles once, when Tracy tapped a little piece of sticky cake onto Faith's nose.

"Try to be professional! You don't see *me* laughing, *do* you?" Tracy huffed.

Watching this exchange, Grace clasped Gabe's hand for temper support as she pressed her lips together.

Bethany arrived to watch practice. Faith soon recovered her composure after a moment, choking down her laughter. Whenever she was under pressure, she had an urge to laugh.

Tracy firmly took her by the arms and plopped her in a chair. However, Tracy's grasp was so hard, it left fingerprint impressions on Faith's arms. Later, Faith slid down and quickly crawled to the floor in search of the doll.

"Too fast, too fast!" cried Tracy, trying to catch up.

"Good job out there; you're very talented," smiled Faith as the scene ended. They were still on the stage and were covered in cold eggs and heavy sweat.

"Thanks." Tracy offered a slight smile.

"What do you have planned for today?" Faith asked.

"My dad is forcing me to go see a photography exhibit at the Detroit Institute of Arts," Tracy sighed. "He thinks it might cheer me up, but nothing makes me happy anymore." She scratched her neck beneath her lace black top. There was a pause. "I *am* a fan of photography, though," Tracy said with a slight upturn of her red lips.

"Do you want to come to TCBY to get frozen yogurt with us?" Faith inquired.

"Nah, maybe next time," shrugged Tracy.

"Oh, okay. See ya." Faith waved.

"At least she smiled. I wasn't expecting any acting affirmations, yet," Faith laughed as she signed to Bethany after practice was over.

"I thought you did great," Bethany said in sign language. "I have to run—I've got dance practice," Bethany said as the gang joined them. With a tap on Caleb's shoulder, Bethany signed to him, getting the attention of the whole group. "Caleb, you are excellent as the angry captain," Bethany signed.

"Hey! What about the rest of us?" Gabe asked as everyone laughed.

"Hey! You got that! That's nice! Oh, sorry.... Let me think..." Bethany began. The gang chuckled softly. "Okay. Gabe, you are a talented Jimmie. Grace, you're a tragic, grieving, but motherly Kate. Faith, you portray Helen as a hopeless tyrant. But at times the audience can feel sorry for the character."

"You got all that from two scenes?" Caleb asked, amazed. Bethany smiled.

"Somebody's got a big performance tomorrow night," Grace said to Bethany. Faith translated for her.

"Yeah, I can't wait for you to come to my performance," giggled

Bethany. Their attention was suddenly directed to Mr. Perry and Tracy, who were talking as they sat down in the auditorium's velvet seats.

"You were great out there, Trace," Mr. Perry said and attempted to high-five her.

"Yeah, thanks," Tracy responded disinterestedly. She walked away toward the auditorium doors.

Grace shook her head. "I just can't stand her."

"She didn't want to get frozen yogurt with us today," Faith said to the gang.

Grace looked relieved and questioned, "Why did you even invite her?"

Faith responded, "It'd be hard to never be invited."

"Caleb and I can join up today for frozen yogurt," Gabe said.

"Yeah, then after, I need to go to basketball practice," commented Caleb.

"Oh, that's right! Thinking of it, you have a big game," Faith interjected with excitement.

"Yeah, we can just pick the tickets up at the ticket booth at the game." Caleb nodded and smiled proudly.

"Also, I've got a choir concert. I was wondering if you'd like to come?" Gabe asked, his eyes looking at Faith eagerly like a hopeful little boy.

"Oh, yeah. I'll write it in my calendar on my iPad," Faith said.

"Hey, Bethany, do you want to join in on Caleb's basketball game?" Gabe asked and then looked at Faith to translate.

"Could we invite Tracy?" Bethany asked. "I agree with Faith. No fun to be left out. Been there."

Grace exhaled and walked away.

"Grace, Tracy's not that bad," Gabe said to her retreating form.

"Do we have to invite her to everything?" Grace retorted.

"Being inclusive just feels right," Faith pointed out, shrugging.

"All right, fine," Grace conceded, huffing.

"Well, guys, I just wanted to come, watch you practice, and support you. I'm going to go to dance now," Bethany smiled.

Chapter Ten

It was a beautiful night with a black sky of twinkling stars and a full moon. A colorful autumn was beginning with a slight chill in the air. The friends entered the historic venue.

"Look how gigantic this theater is!" Gabe exclaimed.

"Here it is," Grace called. "Now which one is it?" She looked at the numbers on the armrests.

"This is so exciting. There's lots of people here," Faith observed.

Caleb sat down, saying, "Here." He patted on the green velvet seat as he pointed to several seats beside him. "Grace, you're there, Gabe there, and Faith here."

About ten minutes later, the lights dimmed as the curtain went up, and "Good News" by Mandisa came on.

Bethany was in a phone booth to stage left. On stage right was an identical phone booth. With the phone to her ear, her mouth was open in surprise. She put the phone back in its stand. Bethany came out of the booth and danced toward a bench at center stage. She put her right foot in front of her left and then stepped back. She slid to the right, rolled her arms, and slid to the left.

Bethany passed behind a bench that had several teen boys sitting there reading newspapers. They had their heads down, hidden behind their papers. As Bethany came behind them, they all lifted their heads in unison. Most of them wore baseball caps and one of them wore a trapper hat. They got phones out from their jackets' pockets. The last young man near the end of the bench gave Bethany a megaphone. They got off the bench and turned around and faced her.

Bethany stood on the bench and pretended to speak into the megaphone, looking at the audience. She moved her shoulders up and down to the beat as she swayed her hips to the music. Bethany gave the megaphone to a boy in the other phone booth to stage right. She did a back handspring off the bench to the right. One of the boys handed her a picket sign, and Bethany raised it above her head. It said in black lettering: "Jesus Loves You." Below it was a red heart.

Leading the dancers, Bethany marched, carrying the sign. The backup dancers had their right hand in salute as if she were the head of a missionary group. Suddenly, they picked up signs with positive messages such as: "Peace be with you! The Lord is my strength and my song. Jesus is my jam. Whom shall I fear? The Lord hears the cry of the poor." They, including Bethany, raised their signs up and down in the air. She tossed her sign to the young man beside her, and immediately crossed her ankles and spun around sharply. She did a front handspring to the right.

Dancing to center stage, she did a grand jete and landed on the bench. Shocking the audience, Bethany flipped backwards off the bench and the air was filled with unanimous cries of surprise and awe. She stopped and a dancer gave her the "Jesus Loves You" sign. She stepped up onto the bench and held it up victoriously. The dance ended there, and she got a standing ovation.

* * *

Crisp and dried leaves rolled, rustled, and murmured across the school parking lot.

In a scene of *The Miracle Worker*, Gabe and Caleb delivered a long, confusing dialogue about the Civil War, while Grace, playing Kate, was supposed to be reading a book. But the book was actually the script that was made into a little book. The actress who played Viney, the cook, served and took away dishes. Meanwhile, Faith was blundering around the table and taking handfuls of food.

Faith and Tracy were struggling as Tracy gripped Faith's wrists painfully.

After several redos of the same scene, Caleb threw down his napkin on the table and said, "Finally, we're done!"

"That speech gets old," Gabe agreed. "All about the Civil War. It's awful to say it over and over again."

"But we did it well, didn't we?" added Faith.

Faith panted and wiped the sweat from her forehead. She got her water bottle and drank to soothe her throat, which was raw from her whimpering and groaning.

The next scene was the Breakfast Scene. There was a lot of wrangling. Faith fake-slapped Tracy, but it was harder than she wanted it to be. Tracy got angry, her eyes glinting fiercely. Tracy raised her hand and slapped Faith's cheek harshly. Faith's cheek stung and throbbed; she wiped her cheek, trying to relieve the pain. By the end of the scene, Faith's legs were sore, her throat scratchy, her palms abraded, and her left cheek stung from the real slap that she had received. Tracy wasn't supposed to do that; it wasn't necessary. In one part of the scene, Annie demands that Helen use a spoon and forces her to get it off the floor. Tracy had taken Faith by the arms, and forced her down, making her muscles sore.

After, Tracy did a scene with Gabe and Grace. It was the scene about Annie trying to convince Helen's parents to let Annie bring Helen to their garden house. The reason? Helen always escaped to them, and that would get in the way of Annie's teaching.

Faith couldn't focus and she had missed several of her cues, so the cast had to start all over again. During scenes, the lines the others had said were forgotten by Faith.

"Why don't you know this?" Tracy asked, annoyed. "We've practiced over and over again."

"I can't think," Faith replied, almost inaudible.

"You're stinking it up! I've had enough!" Tracy shouted.

"Tracy, Faith can't help it if she can't remember because of her seizures," Mr. Perry said. "Dial it down a notch. Let's take five."

An hour later, after the rest of the Breakfast Scene, Faith came up to Tracy and asked, "All of us are going out for dinner. Would you like to join us?" She tilted her head, her eyes shimmering hopefully. She smiled eagerly.

"Sure, why not?" Tracy shrugged.

"Perfect!" Faith giggled her bubbly laugh.

"When is it?" Tracy asked.

"Tonight at six," Faith replied.

Mary woke up in her cot in her cramped sleeping quarters to find her father brushing his teeth with baking soda at the nearby sink across the room. He spat blood into a metal can as he coughed horribly. He was feeble, and had a sickly complexion.

"How are you doing, Dad?" Mary asked.

"Help your ma," Dad replied, stroking his scruffy black beard and pressing his thumb on his cleft chin. He wore baggy pants, a patched cap, and a long coat. He wobbled along, coughing like an old man. He was thirty-five years old. His muscular hands were wrinkly and grimy. His eyes were still young-looking, but he looked care-worn.

"Is your chest pain still ailing you?" Mary asked.

"Yes," replied Dad. "My back and knees are worse, too."

"Oh, Mary, can you tend to the baby?" Mother asked as she scrubbed the breakfast dishes in the sink. Her mother was pallid from lack of sleep and lack of proper nourishment. Mary looked up at her mother's weary forest-green eyes and noticed that her chestnut hair was pulled back in a bun.

"Yes, Mother," Mary obeyed as she kissed her sister Dorothy on the forehead. The baby had glossy, straight, auburn hair that framed her face. She had fair skin, an upturned nose, and dark brown eyes.

"Those small wages you earn are very helpful—I know you don't like going to work," Mother reminded, as she got onto her knees and scrubbed the floor. "We may not have a lot of money, but the money you earn makes all the difference."

"I know," Mary said as she raised her eyes to her mother. Mary recalled that her father had said that her mother was the most beautiful woman he had ever seen—she would definitely be one of those elegant, high-class ladies, her pa had re-marked, had she been born into the upper class.

"Please carry these pails and bring back water from the stream. I need water for your father," said Mother.

"Why are Timothy's clothes in this crate?" Mary asked as she went over to the round, scratched oak table. She picked up the crate full of toddler-sized clothes.

"We should sell your brother's clothes since we're not going to use them. Your baby sister is not a boy," Mother sighed, avoiding eye contact. "Uh...uh.... There's a lot of wear in them. Someone is bound to purchase them."

"Dorothy will be helpful in the fields once she's old enough. I suppose by the time she's four," Dad said.

"Just like Mark's little siblings are doing—picking berries, vegetables, and lifting boxes of produce," Mary agreed.

"Wow!" Caleb exclaimed.

When the friends entered the restaurant, they saw clear strings of lights hung all around the room; they glowed in the dim restaurant. The hubbub of chatter and the merry sound of laughter filled the room. A common country song blared from speakers nearby. A couple, out of sight, clinked their glasses during a toast. At a nearby table, everyone clapped to the music and some of the staff sang "Happy Birthday." Waiters and waitresses bustled around, carrying trays of tastefully presented food. It was tantalizing!

"All right, I showed," Tracy muttered as she approached the table. "It's really dim in here."

Tracy didn't drive with the friends because she wanted to leave early.

"Have you been here before?" Gabe asked.

"Several times, many years ago. My family used to come here," Tracy hesitated. "Back when I was happier." She turned her head to a caterwauling baby. "Think that baby's loud enough?"

Suddenly, a waiter nearly bumped into her.

"Excuse me, miss, my bad," said the waiter in his deep voice.

Tracy said, "Klutz! Oh, of course they had to play country music. I hate this genre!"

Grace exchanged a furtive eye roll with Caleb.

Faith felt energized by the laughter, the chatter, and the mood of the room. Her heart was bursting with joy!

Gabe said, "Country music—I'm not really a fan, but it's okay."

Bethany surveyed her surroundings as the friends picked up their menus.

"Ooh! Saganaki! How about I order that?" exclaimed Caleb.

"No, please don't, Caleb. You know how the smell makes me want to gag and how I hate the fire," Faith remarked.

"Maybe I will," Caleb said jokingly. Faith was radiant as she smiled at Caleb and laughed at his joke.

Faith smelled the fresh aroma of the brightly colored flowers in a vase at the center of the table; she stroked the soft, thick petals. "Cool! These are real!" Faith looked around at her friends. Caleb was telling jokes and laughing hysterically.

"I can feel the vibrations of this song under my feet," Bethany said, signing. She turned to Faith. "Can you look up the lyrics?"

"Can you sign slower? I'm starting to learn a bit, but I only under-stand a few words," Caleb said.

Gabe, Faith, Tracy, Bethany, Caleb, and Grace were in the booth chatting. Everything went smoothly when suddenly...Faith thought, *Oh no, nausea!*

"So I finished the costumes and I'm really proud of them. They're floral, eyelet, and plaid, and they have organza. They're really—" Grace began enthusiastically.

I want to throw up—headache. It's a twinge! Ow! It's okay because it's going to go away soon, Faith thought as she tapped her feet nervously.

"I can't wait to see them! I bet they're your best work yet. I can't sew at all; my grandma tried to teach me but—" Bethany replied in sign, and Faith struggled to keep up.

Tingly foot! Oh great! Okay, pay attention! I want to know what's going on, Faith thought, focusing. She was trying to translate, although the seizure was becoming worse.

"What do you call a cow that plays guitar?" Gabe joked.

Cocking her head, Bethany inquired, "What?"

Gabe, cracking up, finished, "A moo-sician!" Everyone groaned.

"Oh, Gabe." Grace rolled her eyes.

"That's such a dad joke," Caleb commented.

"That's so true. My dad makes jokes just like that," Tracy said.

"Here's a good Catholic joke: What do you call a priest who becomes a lawyer?" Gabe asked.

"What *do* you call a priest who's a lawyer?" Grace asked.

"A father-in-law!" answered Gabe, laughing.

I was hoping I was going to have fun! Dang it! Chest pain! I can't breathe! Yes, you can breathe. What did I just think? Tingling arms! Focus! Faith thought with frustration.

Faith looked down at her arms as her friends discussed their day.

The right corner of my lip jerked. Never mind! Catch up. It'll be okay, reassured Faith to herself.

"How was practice at the dance studio, Bethany?" Caleb asked.

"Oh same old, same old! I'm getting better at this one dance I'm working on, though," Bethany responded.

Bethany has a beautiful smile, Faith thought fondly.

After a short time, Faith, more frustrated, thought, *My foot jerked! My muscle is tense and sore and it hurts. Did they see it? Oh, I hope they didn't! I don't want to ruin the evening!*

Grace asked, "What is your favorite kind of music, Tracy?"

Wait...Grace was being nice! She's trying! Wait...What did I think of? It was something good. It's nice to be here with my friends. They're so pretty and handsome! I love them so much, Faith thought, her seizure easing now.

"I like breakup songs," Tracy said. "I like a clean version of Billie Eliesh's 'Bad Guy' and I like 'Since U Been Gone' by Kelly Clarkson. Um—"

Faith's comprehension of the flowing conversation came to a screeching halt. *Ow! I hate that pelting, burning raindrop sensation against my temple and the back of my head. Never mind that. Keep listening*, Faith thought as she tried to concentrate on what was going on. Her hope was to sign for Bethany and translate what she was signing for the others.

Gabe asked, "What are your favorite—" Faith missed the rest of what Gabe said.

"I like Chaganty's *Run*, Krasinski's *The Quiet Place*, and Lowe's *The Bad Seed*," Tracy replied.

"I've heard of those and saw the trailers, but I'm too scared to see the movies," interjected Faith, trying desperately to join the conversation.

Faith smiled and spoke fluently for one or two minutes. Everything went well for a few moments. Life was good.

Faith thought, *Oh no! I'm nauseated again! Can I have at least one peaceful moment? Don't overreact! People have it worse than you! Ow, my foot! What's going on? What happened?*

Gabe's mouth was moving, but Faith heard no words.

Grace, concerned, asked, "Faith, you—right?" Faith smiled weakly. Grace continued, asking, "Aren't you excited for our play?" Grace's lips were moving. Her eyes were focusing on Faith, and she was animated. Faith heard Grace's voice, but not what she was saying. She sounded excited and she was laughing, but the words were inaudible and couldn't be understood by Faith.

This was important. She's excited about it.... Come on, you don't even know what she said, Faith rebuked herself. *I don't remember. Oh, she's talking about the play! Got it! Good!*

Everything went foggy. Diners whizzed about her, questions were asked, answered, and her friends were very engaged. Things were going on about her, but Faith wasn't aware of it. She heard laughing and chatting, but she wasn't connected to it. Faith was safe, loved, and in a lively environment, but she couldn't participate in the enjoyment.

Faith, aggravated, thought, *Oh, I can't think. I'm getting that hazy feeling. Oh no!*

Grace began, "I always—"

"—Oh really?" Gabe exclaimed, replying to the sentence that for Faith was cut off. He noticed Faith didn't feel well. Gabe locked eyes with her and knew how she felt without even asking.

Faith, feigning wellness, said, "I'm fine."

I'm not fine! You're fibbing to him. But I don't want him to worry.

My seizures happen all the time. Ow, my head! What did I just think? What? Faith thought wildly.

Now she only heard people talking—inklings—and she was too sick to figure it out.

Faith tapped her feet, drummed her fingernails on her knees, and played with her jewelry. Her shoulders, neck, and upper back were tense from seizures.

"I'm sorry," Gabe apologized softly.

I give up! I feel so sick! Why does this always happen? Why can't my seizures just go away? I can never enjoy myself, Faith thought, disheartened.

Gabe whispered, "I'm so sorry. You don't have to listen."

Tracy stayed silent and then said several sentences. Faith could tell it was only a condescending comment by her tone. She was being boastful and gloating about something she knew. It was inaccurate. Faith heard it and knew it was inaccurate, but then it vanished. Now, her friends' voices and their tones were clear, but she didn't understand the meaning. Tracy was almost on mute with barely any clear words.

Suddenly the seizure ebbed, and what Tracy was saying became clear to Faith. "The joke goes like this: A student tells his art teacher, 'Your camera takes really nice pictures.' The teacher replies, 'Thanks, I taught it everything it knows.'" Tracy laughed uproariously. Pointing, she asked, "Are you even listening to what we're saying? Faith, you're not even translating for Bethany."

Faith observed Tracy's angry, arrogant expression and Grace's frustrated face. Surprise was on Gabe's face for a moment.

Grace had brushed off her frustration and continued talking. She was too busy talking to notice what was going on—how Tracy was so angry, how Gabe was trying to help, and how sick Faith was.

"What did you say?" Faith, clearly baffled, asked.

"Never mind—you wouldn't get it. It was nothing," Tracy said nonchalantly.

"Could you please say it slower? You're going too fast," requested Faith.

"My father. Used. To. Take. Home. Videos. Of me with his old camcorder. Is this better? Can you understand this?" Tracy asked.

Great, Tracy's mad! Oh no! So sick! So sick of being tired and miserable. I feel so horrible, Faith thought, distressed.

Bethany signed, saying, "Yeah, I agree with Faith. What did you say? Faith didn't translate right."

Oh great, poor Bethany is missing this because I'm not translating for her.

Tracy, in a irritable tone, said, "Never mind. Why do you care so much about it?" She rolled her eyes. Bethany got out her phone and was in the process of texting Tracy. Hearing the ding, Tracy got out her phone.

Bethany [to Tracy in a group text]: I want to be part of the conversation—just like individuals of the hearing community.

Everyone, hearing their phones indicating a text, got out their phones.

Gabe [to everyone]: Yes, I agree, communication is vital—you know, just like Helen Keller needed communication. For research, I had to learn more sign language and read all about it.

"I also read books...um...articles, videos, and everything. I read all the journals, letters, and writings from Helen Keller," Faith remarked as she concentrated doggedly on her words.

Tracy [to everyone]: Well, were they reputable sources?

She rolled her eyes in a condescending manner.

Tracy: Did you read the sources and double-check their credibility?

She was acting snooty again. Tracy acted like she knew more than Faith. In this instance, Faith knew she had accurate information. Of course, Faith *knew* they were reputable sources. She spent many hours and read loads of information. It was quite a tough blow, and it stung, because Helen Keller was a subject in which Faith was very knowledgeable. Faith clenched her fists, but told herself to calm down.

Tracy: Like, did you know people who are called deaf are completely deaf?

Bethany explained with a serious expression, texting in the group chat: That's not true. We can be profoundly deaf or we might have moderate hearing loss. It depends, really.

Tracy: Well, the good thing about ASL is that it's universal.

Tracy scoffed as she leaned back in her seat with her arms crossed.

Bethany: It's not universal, but it would help if it was.

Bethany offered a playful smile.

Tracy: Well, all people who are Deaf wish they had hearing.

Tracy hurriedly defended herself.

Bethany rectified, texting: No, there is something called Deaf Gain. The Deaf community is tight-knit, and people who are Deaf share their own language.

To change the subject, Faith wanted to ask Tracy a question about music. Faith knew Tracy would say no to whether she liked Christian music or not. But there was a part of her that still hoped she wouldn't be negative about everything. Since Tracy always criticized her, Faith was preparing for disappointment, and an internal eye roll if Tracy said no to her next question. However, she was prepared to perform a mental inward fist launch if she said she *did* like Christian music.

"Do you like Christian songs—" Faith started, but Tracy interjected.

Tracy said, brief and monotoned, "No."

"May I tell jokes?" Gabe cut in, trying to break the mounting tension. Faith only caught inklings of his jokes.

Gabe asked in a whisper, "Hey, Faith, you okay?"

Faith, stumbling over her words, said, "I'm...seizure sick. I'm having a lot of...nausea...um...headaches, numbness, forgetfulness, tingling, tightness...twitching, and jerking. You know, the works."

"I'm sorry. Seizures stink," Gabe said sympathetically.

"Don't stop conversing. You can keep talking without me. I can't listen when I'm seizure sick. I want you to have fun—don't worry about me," Faith told him.

After a while, the seizures got less severe and Faith was able to push past them.

Tracy folded her hands on the table and looked at Faith across from her.

"I can't believe you've been sick this whole time, Faith. Somehow you're happy all the time. Like you see this world, like this beautiful place...full of possibilities, and adventures, and like, friendships." Tracy looked from Faith to Gabe. He was smiling down at Faith. Tracy's eyes filled with tears, and she looked toward the hostess station. "Where's our food?"

* * *

Faith collapsed onto her bed and sighed. She thought about Grace and how she was seething with animosity that Faith was inviting Tracy into the group. Faith tried to give the impression that it didn't bother her that Tracy was always mean to her. She always tried to think on the bright side...but it hurt. All of Tracy's comments were like endless punches to the stomach.

Faith always tried to protect herself—it was armoring up and preparing to go into battle through prayer, and trying to see the positive. Faith didn't know why Grace was so angry. Tracy *was* puzzling, because she found the negative in everything; she was so pessimistic and contrary. No matter what Faith did or tried to do, it didn't seem to matter—Tracy was always in a bad mood.

Faith was only trying to be nice—Grace didn't understand that. The boys and Bethany were her loyal friends, and they were more easygoing. Gabe seemed to be especially faithful to her.

Just then, Faith's phone rang and it was Gabe!

"Hey, are you okay?" Gabe asked.

"I'm doing okay," Faith said.

"I saw Tracy slap you at practice and the *look* in her eyes..." Gabe said as Faith swallowed hard. "Come on, you can be honest with me."

"When Tracy says something mean to the extent that she did in the restaurant, it hurts me. I don't usually say it's painful...but it is," Faith said.

"I'm sorry. You've got Bethany, Caleb, and me if you need to talk. I know Grace doesn't like to talk *anything* about Tracy, that's for sure. But I'm sure Grace will get over it," Gabe reassured as he sighed.

"Okay," Faith said. "Thanks.... How are you?"

"I'm okay," Gabe replied. "I'll see you tomorrow. It'll be okay."

Chapter Eleven

As the dawning sun warmed Mary's back, she lugged two metal pails toward the stream. She spotted Mark squatting down next to it.

"I was merely retrieving water for the troughs for the livestock before work," Mark explained.

"Mother wants to sell Timothy's clothes," Mary remarked as she knelt in front of the stream and looked at her reflection absentmindedly.

"Your family has the worst fortune in the textile mill. First Timothy, and now your dad and his illness."

"That's why they need me." Mary hesitated. "Mother wants to remove all traces of Timothy. He was so young—just a little fella." She choked up. "I can't believe it's been a full year..." She brushed away the tears that were rolling down her cheeks with the back of her hand as she sniffled. "Why did he have to be crushed by one of the power looms? Now, Dad is determined to put Dorothy in the fields as soon as she's able to work. I'm not certain. I can only consider her as a baby at present."

Mark interjected, saying, "I know it's not fair, but that's what my mother wants my younger siblings to be doing—bent over, hefting heavy boxes, and picking for long hours in the sun. Mama can't work in the fields."

"I can't leave my family," Mary said, looking steadily at Mark.

"But you always said the contingency arrangement was that your family would live with your Aunt Nellie. Couldn't they reside there?" Mark asked. "When we find somewhere to live, I shall get a safer job and send money home," Mark nodded.

"I conjecture that's simply the way of the world," sighed Mary. "No matter what we do and how much cruelty or pain we endure, that is how it will be."

"I cannot imagine that your parents would let you retain your job in the textile mill after what occurred with your papa and Timmy," Mark whispered.

"I know, but we need the money, and, of course, we must pay our debt," Mary swallowed a lump in her throat. In the distance, clear and loud, the whistle blew again.

On a dreary autumn day, the friends were in the school auditorium again. They did the Garden House Scene, where Arthur and Kate ride deeply into the country for a long time to confuse Helen. They want her to feel like she's far away, but they return to their garden house on their own property. The Kellers leave her with Annie Sullivan, and Helen has a wild tantrum, knocking everything in her path.

Throughout practice, Faith acted out more sobbing, but it was more of a chest-shaking sob. During this traumatic scene, Faith tapped into deep empathy. She imagined what it would be like to have her beloved parents abandon her—to be trapped in a strange garden house in the middle of nowhere with a demanding teacher, who seemed to force her to do things she loathed. Thinking about those things repeatedly helped Faith to cry and go wild. It was challenging and exhausting, but it was somewhat fun.

After several times of doing the scene, Faith sunk to the floor and took deep, heavy breaths. Sweat beaded down her forehead, and she was thirsty and exhausted.

Tracy's work wasn't as physically demanding, because Annie was just giving Helen a frustrated monologue. The speech was about how she couldn't teach her language.

After practice, Faith went over to Tracy, who was talking to Gabe and drinking her beverage from a dark blue water bottle. They were on the side of the stage.

"Hi, Tracy, want to come to TCBY with Grace and me?" Faith asked.

"All right, you keep asking anyway," muttered Tracy. "Let me just text my mom. My phone is in my duffle. Hold on."

* * *

"What do you wanna get?" Faith asked as she, Grace, and Tracy looked at all the flavors through the glass case. The sunshine reflected in little, white squares on the smooth, cold glass.

"I think I'll get my usual strawberry," Tracy said abruptly.

"I enjoy moose tracks," Faith giggled as she got handed the waffle cone over the counter. She turned to the young employee. "Thank you."

"Mine's cotton candy," Grace said as she licked her pink and blue ice cream.

"What do you like to do?" Faith asked Tracy as they sat down on the magenta plastic chairs around a round, silver metal table.

"Well, I love to take trips with my mom, and I love photography and ice skating," Tracy said.

Internally, Faith was rejoicing that Tracy was acting civil. Grace gave Faith a tentative smile.

* * *

Faith lay in bed, her mind swirling around with thoughts—like clothing in a dryer at the laundromat.

What is my gift? I can't act. Apparently, I'm "stinking it up" and I can't do sports or anything athletic. What's my gift, God? I'm sure You know. Ahh!

Tossing and turning. Left, right, and back again as she heard the tick of the clock in Mom and Dad's room. She checked her phone that was on her lamp table and it said 1:00 a.m. *I want to serve You with the gifts You gave me, but I don't know what they are!*

* * *

The evening sky was streaked with pale pink, a golden orange, and a splotch of purple. It was really beautiful with a still chill in the air. Dad pulled out of the Johnsons' driveway. Faith stood on the porch and waved goodbye to Dad as he left.

"Faith's here!" Mrs. Johnson called down into the basement.

Caleb and Gabe were playing air hockey and Gabe was talking about a philosophy book he was reading.

"I want to become a philosophy professor some day. How about you?" Gabe asked.

"I don't know yet," shrugged Caleb. "A dance instructor or a high school gym teacher...or a Hershey's candy bar taste-tester. Where could I get a job where I could eat all the time?"

"Caleb! That's not even a thing! You just stand in a warehouse and watch the candy go by on a conveyor belt. Then you see if it's okay!" Gabe shook his head, laughing.

"Well, scratch that idea then! Watchin' it go by! That's like a torture! Forget it!" Caleb flicked his wrist. "What about the Skittles company?"

"Same thing, dude!" Gabe replied.

Sitting on the black couch, Bethany was teaching Grace sign. They were communicating some of the words through texting.

"Hey, guys," Faith said as she went down the fresh-lumber basement stairs.

"Hey, Crazy Faith," Caleb chuckled as he came over.

Gabe brightened the moment he saw Faith, but she didn't notice. Bethany looked at Faith and recognized her glum expression.

"What's wrong, Faith?" Bethany asked.

"I was up most of the night thinking and praying to God," Faith sat down on the floor.

"About what?" Caleb asked.

"What is my gift? My thing!" Faith threw her hands in the air dramatically. "I mean, Caleb is the expert athlete, Bethany's an accomplished dancer, Tracy's a talented actress, Gabe's a masterful musician, and Grace's an artistic seamstress. What's my gift? I would love to serve the Lord with my talents, but I don't have any..." She sat down in Mr. Johnson's brown leather recliner.

"That's not true," Gabe objected. "You're an amazing friend."

"Is that even a thing to be had?" Faith asked irritably.

"Sure it is," Gabe said as he sat down on the arm of her chair.

"You just have to have an open mind to possible gifts," Bethany encouraged through sign.

"Tracy says I stink at acting and says I can't remember any of my cues. What do you think?" Faith asked.

"I mean, you're not the *best* at acting, but we can practice at each other's houses. Maybe all you need is more practice and less pressure," Caleb suggested.

"Maybe." Faith bit her bottom lip.

"We wouldn't be able to stand it if you couldn't participate in the play with us," Grace remarked softly. "No, we *need* you. We're in this together until the curtain drops at the final performance."

"Well, that's sweet of you," Faith said as her eyelid twitched and her jaw jerked.

"I didn't find my gift right away—I had to work on my dancing for many years," Bethany explained.

"You're right," Faith smiled.

* * *

Chatter and loud, young people's voices surrounded the teens as they walked through the hallway of the school.

"I'm so excited," Gabe laughed while Faith giggled. "I'm going over to the booth to pay for you guys' tickets." He pointed backwards with his thumb toward the ticket booth.

Overlapping Gabe's sentence, Bethany agreed. "I've been praying for you to feel well today, Faith."

"Thank you," Faith smiled.

"Can we get popcorn?" Grace asked.

"How much did your mom give you?" Faith asked, standing next to Grace. She was looking at Tracy. Faith was holding onto Grace's arm for support.

"Well, we already spent some at Speedway on Slurpees," Tracy reviewed as she leafed through her wallet. "I only have half the amount for the jumbo size of popcorn."

"Don't worry, girls, I can pay the rest," Gabe said.

"Are you sure?" Faith asked.

"I can pay with my money for everyone," Bethany objected.

"No, it's my treat. I don't mind," Gabe said as he grabbed his wallet out of his back pocket.

At the same time, Bethany reached for her purse.

Faith's thumb twitched, her forehead hurt, her left leg stiffened, and her chest felt tight. She wanted to throw up as her arm felt like pins and needles, while her lip twitched. Faith was dizzy and felt like she was going to topple over.

"It's super loud in here," Faith mentioned and covered her ears.

"It's not too loud," Grace said.

"I have that sensory thing, remember?" Faith said. "I have trouble with stinky smells and noises. I think annoying noises are louder than they are. I also think stinky smells are potent. Like cheese smells like—"

"No, don't talk about it," Grace said, scrunching up her nose.

"I have headphones in my bag. Do you want them?" Gabe asked.

"No, thank you. I can ignore it," Faith said.

"Do you want them in the gym?" Gabe asked, reaching into his bag to grab them. "It's going to be super loud with the screaming, whistling, and cheering."

Gabe's so sweet and considerate of my well-being, Faith thought as she tried to hide a smile. *But he doesn't "like me" like me.*

"I can just ignore it," Faith said.

The game was going well, but Faith couldn't see anything. The jersey-wearing players were blurry to Faith.

Pointing at the boys in the blue jerseys, Gabe spoke directly into

Faith's ear, saying, "Caleb's team is in purple. They're against the boys in blue."

"Those guys are pretty cute," Grace giggled. Faith nodded absent-mindedly, but translated it for Bethany, who smiled.

"What's happening? Where's Caleb?" Faith asked.

"Over there. He's the tall, fast one. See that wild guy with the black hair?" Grace pointed to the boy in the front. Boys in blue jerseys crowded around him. The squeaking of tennis shoes, whistling, cheering, and yelling echoed through the gym. Faith covered her ears and squinted at the blurry boys.

* * *

"Hey, guys." Caleb bounded toward them. He was sweaty and had just come from the game.

"Dude, you rocked." Gabe high-fived Caleb.

"You did well!" Faith smiled.

"You should've seen how you looked out there. I know you can't really get the whole picture when you're busy playing!" Grace exclaimed.

"You're a basketball extraordinaire," Bethany signed.

"Thanks, I think I got most of that." Caleb smiled at Bethany.

"*Extraordinaire* is probably the word you missed. I'll be right back. I need to use the restroom," Faith said and turned toward the lockers.

"All right, we'll be in the gym. Then we'll be in the commons," Caleb remarked.

"The bathrooms that we usually use are going to be packed. There'll be a huge line," Grace said.

"Oh, I don't mind," Faith said with a flick of her wrist.

"Nah, I don't want you to wait," said Caleb. "Go use the other one. Go forward—past this hallway, then turn right and past more lockers. Later, turn right after the lockers again."

"There's artwork and there's the trophy case. You can't miss it," Gabe clarified.

"Okay, be right back," Faith said as she surveyed her surroundings. She knew she might forget how to get back. Then, Faith simultaneously tried to memorize what Caleb said about where the friends would be afterward. *Left? Right? Artwork? Trophy case? Where was it?* As she went further, Faith forgot the directions. It was taking a longer time to find the bathroom than she'd expected. Everything looked the same—same tile, purple lockers, and white-painted walls. It was extremely confusing.

"Faith, are you here? Is everything okay?" Gabe's voice echoed through the empty hallway. "Are you okay? Did you, like, find the bathroom?" Gabe asked as he walked toward Faith.

"I didn't find it. I got a little lost, that's all," Faith shrugged. "I hope I didn't keep you waiting too long."

"No, not at all. Here, I'll show you to the bathroom, and we'll go back together," Gabe offered.

"Thank you," Faith sincerely said.

Faith and Gabe found the bathroom.

"Ready?" Gabe asked as he leaned up against the tile wall outside of the bathroom. Gabe took a little drink from the water fountain.

"Yep," Faith said as she exited the bathroom.

"Where have you two been? It's been ten minutes!" Grace exclaimed. Gabe gave his cousin a look that said not to complain.

"I agree," Tracy grumbled. "Took forever!"

"She got a little lost," Gabe said good-naturedly. "Remember, Grace, Faith doesn't go to this school. She knows where the auditorium is, but not this side of the school."

"I'm sorry to keep you waiting," Faith apologized.

"That's okay. All is forgiven," Grace smiled. Bethany, Caleb, and Tracy nodded in agreement.

Soon, they were all congratulating Caleb and the rest of his buddies on their victory. They exited the school and Tracy rolled her eyes, saying, "I think that's enough congratulating. Seriously, they were cheering him on from the time he got out of uniform to the time we got into the parking lot."

"Dairy Queen, everyone?" Caleb asked, laughing.

"Actually, for once, sounds great to me," Tracy chuckled. "I'm out of cash."

"Yeah, us too," Grace said.

"No problem. I can buy for my fandom, who's expensive," Caleb chuckled.

As the sun came up on Mark and Mary's very rare day off, they were sitting in front of the house, talking.

"Come to the pasture—I want you to see something." Mark took Mary by the hand and they headed toward the fenced pasture. They walked toward a ewe and her lamb. "Look who was born today," Mark said as he pulled the lamb into his arms.

"Oh my!" Mary breathed. "When?"

"At dawn," Mark replied as he sat down beside her. Mary pet the soft wool as the baby lamb baaed. "What should we call him?" Mark asked as he gave her a playful grin.

"David—it means beloved," Mary said, looking at Mark. "What a beautiful creation from God."

"Don't you ever try to escape me! You hear? Useless lass!" The overlooker gripped a young girl by the ears and shook her violently. She was slapped across the face with such vehemency that blood dribbled down her upper lip. She was then ordered to walk up and down the aisles as everyone watched in horror. The overlooker dragged her up the stairway toward the loft. Mary and Mark exchanged a furtive, terrified look.

"See what happened to her? Let'er be an example for all of ya if you try to ever leave," said the overlooker.

Just then the whistle pierced through the midday air, announcing luncheon.

Standing by the window with Mary, Mark encouraged her as they drank their milk, whispering, "Do not fret, we shall persevere and find another way. We could leave before the sunrise—before the whistle blows." He nodded understandingly and remarked, "I know you don't want to leave. But I couldn't bear it if you were ever beaten by the overlooker. He's a variety of dishonorable traits—cruel, abusive, and lecherous. I care about you too much. I've seen what the overlooker has done to some girls your age."

"Thank you. You've endured hardships and abuse from him as well," Mary said. "I know you speak the truth, Mark."

After hours of toiling at the same tasks, the whistle sounded, allowing the workers to return home.

"I must prepare supper for my family. I shall see you tomorrow." Mary smiled at Mark.

As Mary ran home that evening, rain pelted on her head and thunder sounded through the clouds. She could barely keep her eyes open, but she was used to functioning on only a meager amount of sleep.

God, tell me what to do—I don't want to forsake my family by abandoning my job, but I want to live far away from the mill. I want to fulfill my vocation of being a wife and a mother. I can't continue in this manner, even though I know I must for my family, Mary prayed. *Please help Mark...I loathe seeing him in such agony, but he denies his pain, which is evident. I ask, Lord, that I could be with him for the rest of my life. I pray I could see him thrive where the claws of the overlooker or the mill could never touch him. Amen.*

Perhaps Mark is correct—perhaps we could escape. Somehow...

Mary entered the dark house as she opened the chipped and splintered wooden door that hung loosely on its hinges.

"Hello, dear," Mother said as she sat at her normal place at the kitchen table. Although the kitchen was spotless, there were cracks in the kitchen walls.

Mary helped her mother with the baby and helped serve the soup, and then Mary sliced the bread.

"Will you set the child in her crib?" Mother asked her.

"Yes, Mother," Mary said. What if Mark and I were successful at our plan? We could be married and would live a happy life.

"I know your sixteenth birthday is tomorrow—I regret that you must work all day," Mother said as she walked to her sewing basket and brought out a handkerchief with a large blue daisy embroidered on it. "It's made from one of Timothy's shirts."

"Oh, Mother! It's grand!" cried Mary as she threw her arms around her mother. Her eyes welled with tears.

The next day, Faith, Bethany, and Grace were in Grace's room. Grace was laughing and was very talkative.

"I wish you felt well. Why do you always say you're fine when you're sick?" Grace asked.

"I mean, I don't want to complain and I want to have a cheerful, optimistic perspective, you know? I mean, I try not to complain if I can help it." Faith pressed her lips together as her right arm jerked. "It's such a small...ow—thing." Faith faked a smile.

"Why do you always say that?" Grace asked sharply.

"What?" Faith asked, absentmindedly, snapping out of a daze.

"Say you're fine when you're not. It's obvious that you just had a seizure," Grace said.

"My seizures come and go. One moment I'll feel well and then a seizure will come on like gangbusters. I'm not very good with time, but my mom and dad say each seizure lasts a few minutes," Faith explained.

"Grace, please," Bethany said with a soft expression and held up a hand. She turned to Faith. "Well, we're here for you."

"Especially Gabe," Grace teased, laughing.

"Oh, come on, stop it," Faith laughed. "But seriously, I don't want him to worry about me. I mean, I don't want to bother him with all my drama." Faith blew air through her lips. "I want to appear happy. Sometimes, at home, I can relax when I feel like I don't have to put on a smile. But seizures are exhausting, so I try not to talk about it all the time."

"We aren't happy *all* the time," Bethany pointed out.

Faith said, "I want to have fun, but most of the time I feel ill. I want to communicate with friends, but most of the day I feel awful. I feel drained, confused, and gross. The spirit is willing, but the flesh is weak. It takes the fun out of most things. I manage, but I do get sick of it! I can't get up for early activities. I won't be able to drive like you guys all will, because I have a visual impairment and seizures. I can't see far away, in the dark, and my field of vision is so small. I shouldn't be talking about this. I should just focus on happiness," Faith said as the area below her right eye jerked. "Like right now, talking about it, I feel like a whiny baby."

"It's okay to express what's going on with you," Bethany signed.

Faith's fingers trembled as one of her legs jerked. The right corner of her lip twitched. "Don't sit there and watch me. I'm done. Get up and dance. I know you want to, Grace. The music always cheers me up, although it doesn't make the seizures better."

"What's the next move to help your seizures?" Bethany interjected.

"I'm going to the hospital," Faith said.

"Why do you have to go to the hospital?" Grace whined.

"For an EEG and some scans," Faith said.

"We'll visit you. I'm sure the boys will go and support you, too," Bethany remarked in sign language.

"Let's dance." Grace leaped up and played upbeat Christian music. Faith sat up and watched as she clapped to the beat. She was so dizzy. "Come on, dance!" Grace encouraged as Faith's left foot jerked. Faith just shook her head no and waved Grace off.

"Hey, girls! Faith, you look a lot better since the last time I saw you. Did the seizure pass, or are you ignoring it?" Mrs. Foster asked as she came into Grace's room with a laundry basket under her arm.

"No, it's there," Faith said as she began to feel exhausted and as if she couldn't go on with the day. But she forced herself.

"Oh... You *look* fine," Mrs. Foster said. "Maybe you'll feel better after you eat something."

"Thanks." Faith offered a wavering, feeble smile. *I wish she wouldn't say that, but I know she's trying to help. It's so annoying when people think certain things will make a seizure stop.*

"Oop! The boys must be here. I heard the doorbell." Mrs. Foster walked hurriedly down the hall to open the door for Gabe and Caleb.

After talking to Bethany and Grace for a while, Faith went into the kitchen and poured herself a glass of water at the sink. Gabe noticed her and stopped her to talk.

"Hey, Faith, how are you feeling?" Gabe asked, his voice chipper.

"To be honest with you, not so well. I hate to always tell you that, because I don't want you to worry about me. I just...I don't want your focus to be on me not feeling well all the time." Faith's brown eyes were downcast.

"That's okay. You can always tell me how you're doing when you're sick. I don't want you to lie to me when that's not the truth." Gabe gave Faith a casual smile. "I know you can't help feeling sick."

"Thanks, Gabe. You can tell me, too, if you're not feeling well," Faith returned. *Way to wreck it, Faith*, snickered Faith to herself. *I just wanted to return some kind of gesture. As if he would want that. Way to go....*

"Thanks," Gabe said. "Hope you feel better." He smiled at her. "It's not fun, and it ruins your quality of life. I don't have seizures, but I can empathize, and I try to understand what it's like. I'm not happy when others aren't happy," Gabe explained.

"Excuse me. I'm going back to my friends," Faith said.

"What am I? A book?" joked Gabe.

Chapter Twelve

Bells chimed in the elevator as it stopped at the children's pediatric neurology floor. Faith was welcomed warmly by the hospital staff. She and her father were shown to the private hospital room, and Faith carried some bags while Dad got the suitcase.

"Looks like she's moving in. She's bringing everything but the kitchen sink," Dad joked, chuckling. Faith blushed and shrugged sheepishly.

Faith brushed her bright red hair and put it in little braids, which was to prevent tangles. If she did get tangles, she would lose lots of hair.

Mr. Tom, whose job it was to apply the electrodes, told Faith about his dog while he marked her head with a red marker for placement of the electrodes. The glue he applied to her head was goopy and smelled horrible. He stuck the electrodes on and added more glue as necessary. Mr. Tom blew air on the glue with what reminded Faith of an air gun. She had to breathe through her mouth to not smell the bad scent.

After Mr. Tom was done, Faith ordered lunch from the hospital menu. She was glad when her tray came.

"Hey, Faith," Gabe whispered as he knocked on the door.

As all her friends filed into the room, Faith pushed her tray away in surprise.

"You all came?" Faith asked in disbelief.

"I thought you'd be out of your pajamas," Tracy grumbled. Grace nodded in agreement.

"You have to wear *pajamas*? I'd be *so* embarrassed!" Grace said, looking mortified.

"It's easier to get ready with something that buttons down the front," Faith remarked.

"Caught you on a bad hair day," Caleb laughed.

Faith's hair was in little braids. Her head was wrapped in a turban made of gauze. She had surgical tape all across the turban. Twenty colorful electrodes were attached to her head and were plugged into a box in a blue Velcro bag.

"Can I unpack for you?" Gabe offered softly. Bethany sat on Faith's hospital bed.

"No, you don't have to," Faith said from her reclining position.

"No, we'll help," Grace persisted.

"I'll do the clothes since Faith probably wouldn't want *boys* rummaging through her clothes," Tracy said to the boys over her shoulder. She went across the room and sat down.

"I'll do the bathroom stuff," Grace said.

"What can I do?" Caleb asked. "How can I help?"

"Caleb, are you hungry? I ordered a cookie. Dark chocolate, your favorite." Faith held out a cookie.

"Mmm." Caleb licked his upper lip. "You're not hungry for it?"

"No, I'm full," Faith declined. "The pot roast here is awesome. Their green beans also rock."

"I didn't know they had good hospital food here. I thought all hospital food stunk," Grace said.

"They have their own greenhouse here. Can you believe it?" Faith mentioned.

"Oh, wow! That's super cool," Caleb said and then turned toward the large window. "This view from your window is boring—it's just buildings' roofs."

"Yeah, most hospitals I've been to for tests have just boring views of dirty streets, or sides of brick buildings," replied Faith. "I feel badly that I'm not offering you anything, Bethany. Do you want ice cream? I got some vanilla and chocolate?" she signed to Bethany.

"Ooh! Yes, please. Are we even allowed to have your food?" Bethany asked in sign, reddening.

"Maybe we shouldn't take her food. We don't want to steal it from her, and plus, what if someone walks in, like a nurse or doctor or something, and we're all here snacking and gorging on Faith's food?" Gabe asked.

"I am quite the foodie," Caleb said. "Gabe, don't be such a dad."

"Who cares? They'll just toss it anyway if we don't eat it," Grace said.

"Grace, do you want my pineapple slices? I already ate some of the green beans, so you probably don't want those."

"I don't want pineapple slices, but what else have you got?" laughed Grace.

"It's like, um...the multiplication of the loaves and fishes," said Caleb. "The food just keeps comin' and comin'."

"You barely ate your beans. Did you just pick at them?" Tracy remarked, her palms facing the ceiling as she gestured to the vegetables.

"Ooh! Who's the parent now?" Gabe asked.

"Ha, ha!" laughed Tracy.

"Oh, I was nauseated," Faith said as her stomach growled. She put some green beans in her mouth and wanted to gag, but held the veggies in as she waited for the nausea to stop.

"Where's Mr. Daniel?" Gabe asked.

"He's in the cafeteria," replied Faith.

A brief knock sounded on the door. "Hey, there's only supposed to be two visitors at a time. Sorry," said the timid nurse from the doorway.

"I thought since Faith had a private room, we could all join in," Tracy said to the nurse. Tracy turned to her friends. "We'll switch around," she shrugged. "Caleb, Grace, and I can go into the cafeteria for a half hour."

"We'll get you something," Caleb said while getting up to exit the room. "We stole it all! Some visitors we are!"

The friends all laughed and Tracy and Grace followed Caleb.

"My dance recital is coming up. Do you want to come, guys?" Bethany asked in sign. "I already invited the others."

"Wow! I hope I can go," Faith said.

"Oh, that's super exciting. Where is it?" Gabe asked.

"At the theater venue downtown," Bethany signed.

"It's really fancy there. I've been there when I was younger. I love it there. It's so beautiful," Gabe said.

"When is it, Bethany? Let me just write down the date of your recital, 'cause I'll forget." Faith quickly set reminders in several apps. "Oh, it's very close to your choir concert, Gabe. Right before. I have that on the calendar. See?" Faith got her iPad from her tray and gave it to him.

"Oh, yeah." Gabe looked down at the dates and smiled. Bethany, Gabe, and Faith decided to scroll through Faith's iPad to find something to watch, because the hospital TV didn't work very well. They settled on *The Sound of Music*, and had just reached the part where Maria is meeting the von Trapp children, when Grace, Tracy, and Caleb came back into the room.

"Switch!" Grace said impatiently, and sat down next to Faith. She immediately started talking, oblivious to the fact that the others were watching a movie.

"Hey, guys," Caleb said, interrupting Grace's monologue. "This movie's a classic. Sorry we interrupted it." He looked pointedly at Grace.

"That's okay," Faith said, pausing the movie.

"No biggie," Bethany signed.

"We've seen it before—like a million times," Gabe said. There was a short hesitation.

"Hopefully, we can get back to band practice soon. We haven't played for the congregation for a long time," Grace thought aloud.

"I can't really plan anything right now. But I'd like to start again," Faith said.

"Yeah, she's a little bit busy right now," Tracy scoffed.

"Grace told me in the car on the way here how Gabe is getting his driver's permit soon," Bethany signed.

"Yeah, pretty soon. No big deal," Gabe said.

"Congrats! I'm so happy for you. What a big accomplishment!" Faith exclaimed.

"Hopefully, there'll be a self-driving car soon, so you can get yours, Faith," Caleb said.

"What are you talking about?" Tracy asked. "Why does Faith need a self-driving car? Can't she just drive a regular one like me? Is it because she has epilepsy? I know people with uncontrolled epilepsy can't drive because it can be dangerous."

"That's one reason. I can't see well due to my CVI," Faith commented. "So, I have *two* reasons why I can't drive."

"I've never heard of CVI," Tracy shrugged. "What is it?"

"Didn't you say CVI is brain-related?" Gabe asked.

"Cortical Visual Impairment—CVI. That means I have trouble seeing, but it's caused by my brain damage, not my eyes. My eyes are perfectly healthy. I always say, 'My eyes are useful, but undependable.' I can't see stairs correctly when I look down. I have no peripheral vision. Some cement stairs, like the ones at church, just look like pavement when I look down. So, I use the tip of my toe or my heel to feel the next step.

"I can't see in the dark, like when I walk through a dark hallway—I have to use touch to get around. I can't see on either side of me. I just see blurs of bright colors instead of figures out of the corners of my eyes; I have to completely turn my head. I can't see far away, either. When my parents and I are in the car, they have to stop the car completely for me to see Christmas lights, an animal, or a house or something. When someone walks by and smiles at me, I don't notice, because it happens too fast," Faith explained.

"So, you need to focus in on it." Tracy nodded with understanding.

"I can drive you places," offered Gabe.

Faith laughed.

"Okay, only two at a time, guys," the nurse said, coming back into the room.

"Okay, we're goin'," Gabe replied as Bethany got up.

"I guess I'm banished again, too," Caleb said.

* * *

It was very beautiful weather on the succeeding day, because the sky was clear and the leaves had changed to auburn, orange, yellow, and gold.

Sun streamed through the large rectangular window. Faith awoke, overly warm and uncomfortable from the gauze over her ears. Covered by heavy coarse blankets, Faith raised her eyes to the camera that was watching her. She glanced at the monitor that had beeped and had recorded her brain waves in bright blue and dark red. Mom sat reading on the shiny, thin recliner. Nurses and physicians had been whizzing in and out of the room all day. Faith had just finished schoolwork and then had taken a nap.

Mom handed Faith her tablet. She had been using it while Faith was sleeping. Faith was in bed in her pajamas that buttoned down the front, since she couldn't pull a top over her head.

"From your friends," clarified Mom.

The video began. There was a black screen that said in white letters "Oh My Love" by The Score.

A close-up shot of the boys at Caleb's house in the living room showed on Faith's screen. Caleb was tapping his drumstick on one of the cymbals.

Tracy was clapping her hands while Bethany was snapping her fingers. Grace was shaking and tapping a tambourine.

Gabe was in front of Caleb singing into a microphone; he was holding onto its stand. Tracy was singing the chorus part, Bethany was signing the lyrics, and Gabe was pointing at the camera as he sang. The video was made of multiple cuts—now Gabe was shown picking up a guitar and strumming it.

In the next scene, Caleb was wearing sunglasses and singing into a wooden, wire hairbrush. He was doing The Moonwalk as the girls were singing into perfume bottles with the caps on. Suddenly, hilariously, the Johnsons stepped into the camera view and Mr. Johnson spun his wife. Faith covered her eyes embarrassedly, and then she giggled with pleasure.

Grace, Tracy, and Bethany were squatting behind the couch, their chins resting on the back of it. Caleb did a front flip and landed on one of the cushions. He crossed his legs and shook his foot and looked casually into the camera.

Bethany did a pirouette, her arms in a teacup rim position.

Caleb did The Worm and then he stood and everyone joined hands. They did The Wave. They all jumped and there was a snapshot of them in mid-air.

The video ended with everyone holding up a sign that said: "We miss you! We love you!"

Smiling warmly at the dark screen, Faith turned to her mom, and exclaimed, "I can't believe they took the time to make a whole video for me!"

Faith picked up her phone immediately and called Grace.

"What did you think?" Grace asked enthusiastically.

"It was beautiful. That was amazing! It must have been very fun to film," laughed Faith.

"It was. Caleb and Bethany came up with the choreography. Gabe, Tracy, and I came up with the shots and the main idea. It was a fun day," recalled Grace. "Next time, you'll be in it."

As the rooster sounded the alarm in the wee hours of the morning, Mary had already set out into the woods to gather water
from the stream. Kneeling at the stream's edge and sinking her
feet into the cool water, Mary dumped the wooden bucket into
the rippling stream as she closed her eyes, enjoying a peaceful
moment.

She heard Mark's voice, saying, "Hello, Mary. I know it's your
birthday today, so I have something for you."

Mary started as she whirled around, drawing her feet out of
the water. "What's that behind your back?"

Mark was holding some purple and red flowers. "Here, I just
picked them in the field over there. I didn't arrange them prop-
erly, though." Mark outstretched his hand that clenched a fistful
of wildflowers as he looked down at his feet. "My father never
used to pick flowers for my mother—he was too consumed at
the mill for such conventions. I don't know if you care for frivo-
lous gestures of affection."

"They're lovely, and I am awfully fond of bellflowers. I love
flowers—even though no young gentleman has ever given me
any." She smiled up at Mark. He looked so handsome with his
soft and errant hair blowing in the breeze. "I don't know how to
thank you enough."

"No need—your grateful expression suffices." Mark held up
his hand. "Sorry for my unruly appearance. I was helping my
siblings with their chores." He scratched some dirt off his fore-

head; his bare feet were covered in swampy mud, and flowers' leaves stuck to his skin.

Mary and Mark shared a gentle gaze for a long moment, and then they both turned slightly red in the cheeks.

"If we were going to escape, how would it be done?" Mary asked.

"So you've given it some thought?" Mark raised his eyebrows.

"Yes, I want to get away from the mill. I…I want to get married and have children—and live far away from the overlooker. I want my parents and sister to be secure."

"And I've been giving it much thought as well." He walked closer to her. "I was composing a plan in my mind last night."

"What is it?" Mary asked, sitting down under an oak tree. She gestured beside her.

"Well, I was thinking—perhaps in the middle of the night we could change out of our night attire and into other clothes fit for such an excursion as this. We must escape before the sun comes up, and before the whistle blows…. We'll meet in the woods when it's pitch black out—I shall explain it further in a moment. As you are aware, the mill owner will ensure that we remain in large debt if we keep paying him. He wants an excessive amount of money—the sum keeps getting larger and larger. If I get a safer job and we live with our families, we will be able to keep my earnings. We will have enough food to eat."

"What's the matter, Mark?" asked Mary, observing him looking down despairingly at his lap. She laid a hand gently on his shoulder.

Mark looked up at her with such meaning and intensity, saying, "We have to make sure no one catches us—even our own family."

Dark purple, orange, golden, magenta, and light pink sunlight streaked the sky as it streamed through the hospital window. Two physicians exited the room. Someone knocked at the door with his fist as he poked his head into the room.

"Hey, may I come in?" Gabe asked as he hugged something brightly colored close to his chest.

"Gabe, you came! So wonderful to see you," Faith smiled welcomingly. The nurse, meanwhile, was taking Faith's pulse, and put the heart monitor on her. She threw away a set of electrodes and attached another. The nurse replugged the red, black, and white wires of Faith's adhesive heart monitor into a plug. She wrapped a bandage around Faith's finger, and red light shone through the bandage. The nurse was so accustomed to doing these procedures that it took her only a few seconds.

"I'd hug you, but my electrodes and my heart monitors are connecting me to *the wall*."

"Where's your dad?" Gabe asked.

"Dad's in the cafeteria, because he's feeling kinda snacky. He's looking for Cheetos, Doritos, Fritos, and Tostitos. He's looking for something with 'eeto' at the end," Faith said. The nurse was taking Faith's temperature.

"These are for you." Gabe handed Faith a bouquet of bright red tulips.

"Oh, you got me flowers! Thank you so much," Faith said graciously.

"Those *are* beautiful," the nurse interjected with a raise of her eyebrows.

"You're welcome, Faith.... You're in my prayers, you know. Bethany and Grace told me they're also praying for you," Gabe said.

"Aww! Thanks! It means a lot. Prayer is powerful," Faith said. "It's been crazy here."

"Looks like it. There's lots of nurses, assistants, and doctors coming in and out of this room. Are they asking you a lot of the same questions?" Gabe asked.

"Yeah, they do, but it's okay," Faith shrugged.

"I know you're super busy. Is it okay that I'm here again?" Gabe asked.

"It's actually nice to have visitors who aren't medical people," Faith explained.

The nurse took her blood pressure and then smiled and left the room.

"Have a great visit, you two," the nurse said.

"Hang in there, Faith. God will heal your seizures in time," Gabe assured as he looked at her. In addition to the seriousness, his eyes expressed affection and admiration.

"I believe He will, too," Faith smiled, lifting her head as she gazed up at him.

Faith touched the back of her neck in a nonverbal and subtle complaint of pain. She inhaled softly.

"I was doing pretty well today." Faith brushed off the discomfort. Gabe sat down on the edge of her bed.

"Caleb told me you couldn't eat your lunch slash dinner. It was—" Gabe began.

"What did you say?" Faith asked, muddled. The ending was forgotten by Faith because of her seizures.

Gabe continued, "It's been tough."

"It's better than normal seizure. Average—it's not too bad and it's not minor, either." Faith sat up straighter.

"Yeah, but you've had terrible nausea," Gabe reasoned.

"I've had medium nausea and a few gaggy-feeling moments," Faith said optimistically. The right corner of Faith's lip twitched and her right arm jerked. She sighed. "It gets tiresome. I know I'm perfectly healthy despite my seizures," Faith pointed out.

"Yes, it's an invisible chronic illness. Another reason why it stinks," Gabe said.

Faith looked down at her arm, saying, "It's uncomfortable." She held her arm as worry made her brows knit together.

"Wish you didn't have it," Gabe said softly.

"Thanks. So sick of it," Faith said as she clenched her jaw.

"You'll be okay. I'm sorry you have to go through this," Gabe said. "You wanna pray about it?"

"May we pray now?" Faith requested.

"Sure." Gabe bowed his head and folded his hands. "God, help Faith. Help her seizures to get better. Please, You're the Almighty Healer." Gabe lowered his head. He put his forehead to his hands that were pressed together. They crossed themselves and ended the prayer.

"Seizures are a concealed battle..." Faith whispered. "Thank you for the flowers."

I love having Gabe with me. He's so sweet, goofy, and just amazing. I love that he understands my pain, even though he doesn't have epilepsy.

"Let's not talk about seizures anymore. On a happier note, where do you want to live?" Faith asked.

"Um...in the woods," Gabe said.

"I would love that, too," Faith agreed. "I feel like the world's progress has ruined our earth with buildings. At a time in the early 1900s, it was beautiful and the structures were few. I saw it in an old film."

"Yes, I agree with that. I'm a big fan of trees, too," Gabe laughed. "Hmm...I would absolutely give anything to live in the woods because of nature and like...the solitude," Gabe explained.

"Well, the solitary life is sure not for me—I wouldn't be content without anyone to converse with," Faith commented. "But I'd enjoy being surrounded by the plants, peace, and creatures, you know? It'd be cool to live in an Edwardian mansion."

"It'd be pretty awesome, but usually they would be really old and they need to be fixed," Gabe said.

"Maybe I could have a new one built that looks Edwardian," Faith offered.

"Maybe—did you find any other philosophy questions for us to talk about?" Gabe asked with a playful smile.

Faith grabbed her iPad and started to scroll through the various questions. "Umm...let me see.... If you could change anything about the world, what would it be?" Faith recited from the philosophy questions she had saved.

Gabe cried, "Unity!" as Faith said, "World peace!"

"Crazy how we think alike," Gabe laughed.

"Today, the doctor said brain surgery would be extremely difficult, because they don't know exactly where my seizure activity is. I have what they call irritative zones, or places where seizures are likely to start, in multiple areas," Faith explained with a dispirited sigh. "Sorry I just burst out with that. It's been on my mind."

"Faith...that's so disappointing. I don't know what to say." Gabe touched her hand supportively. He hesitated as he searched for words. "I know you were really hoping that this surgical workup would be worthwhile, and would qualify you as a surgical candidate."

"I'm processing it on the inside. I haven't talked about it that much. I cried a little, but I'm waiting on the Lord. I'm hoping for a miracle from Him, or a more advanced procedure to come out. I'm more worried about my short-term memory," Faith said softly. "I have strong faith in the Lord. I'm just waiting on God."

"I'm so, so sorry. I know you're in daily pain and it stops you from having fun," Gabe said. "I'll keep praying for you."

"Thank you," Faith whispered as she looked down at Gabe holding her hand.

"I'm sorry. I didn't mean to disturb you or anything," a male nurse said as he came into the room and stuck a needle into one of Faith's electrodes and inserted cold gel into it.

Romance killer, thought Faith to herself.

Dad walked into the room and sat down at the window seat, sticking his hand into a bag of Doritos and crunching noisily.

Noo! Go back to the cafeteria, and search high and low for more 'eetos,' Faith smiled to herself.

"We're ready to take Faith downstairs to the adult floor to have her MRI," said a nurse, appearing in the doorway. She had her thick, frizzy hair back in a ponytail and wore scrubs patterned with bold flowers.

"Almost done here," said the male nurse, who was adjusting the electrodes.

"I'm just starting my shift, Faith. I'll see you when you get back upstairs," the female nurse said.

"I should probably go," Gabe said and stood. He bent over and quickly hugged Faith.

A male nurse came into the room. He wore blue scrubs and was balding; he had a little bit of black hair and had dark, chocolate-colored skin. He rolled Faith's bed down the hall and into an elevator. After going down several floors and through a double-door, he began a short conversation about his golden retriever.

Once in the cold MRI room, the female technologist told Faith that she could choose a movie to watch during the forty-minute scan. Faith warned them that she would involuntarily jerk or twitch.

"Since you can't help that—that's just something we'll have to live with," a young, male, bearded nurse said. Covered with a blanket, Faith lay on the table with her head propped on a pillow. The nurses put two cushions to the sides of her head as they put goggles over her eyes. Then they covered her up with two warm blankets and made sure she was comfortable.

As they put her into the machine, they explained she would be able to see the movie on a screen through the goggles. Faith was excited about the prospect of watching a movie while having this lengthy procedure. Unfortunately, for some reason, the movie was on mute, and so

Faith opted to watch the movie silently rather than bother the techs. If she needed the nurses, Faith was told to squeeze a rubber ball contraption at her side. Faith almost fell asleep because she was so cozy. However, she did have to adjust to the churning sound, and there was an occasional bang that she didn't like. It was kind of like being in a dryer.

When she got out of the MRI, Mom was reading in the waiting room, and Dad said he was leaving. He kissed Faith on the forehead, and they said their goodbyes.

After bloodwork, Faith was wheeled into another room to have a CT scan. She again lay on a table, and the technician put cushions on either side of Faith's head. While she was inside the machine, Faith distracted herself by playing the first episode of one of her favorite shows, *Best Friends Whenever*, in her head. She knew it by heart.

For lunch the next day, Faith was eating a very good turkey and salami sandwich. She got a text from Bethany.

Bethany: How are you?

Faith: I'm okay today. Are you coming to the next rehearsal?

Bethany: I'll try—I'm really busy with dance next week, but I want to be there to see you guys. Love you! Gotta go!

Faith: 'Kay.

A few hours later, Faith got a text from Grace.

Grace: Are you coming to Bethany's dance recital?

Faith: Yep! So excited! Are you?

Grace: Yeah, I'm sorry I can't come to see you. I've gotta lot of homework.

Faith: That's okay.

She received a text message from Gabe.

Gabe: Hey, Faith. How ya feelin'?

Faith: Okay, but not great.

Faith thought Gabe knew what that meant.

Gabe: I'm sorry to hear that. How is it going at the hospital?

Faith: I'm about to read with Mom. I really like the kind nurses.

Later, Faith and Mom sat on a hard bench—which was kind of like a window seat—that looked out over the hospital grounds. They decided to do some schoolwork with Faith's downtime. Together, they alternated reading parts of *The Scarlet Letter* and *The Silent Spring*. Reluctantly, Faith worked on some math.

Faith bookmarked her spot in *Jane Eyre* after she heard a knock at the door. She was annoyed, because she was really into her book.

"Come in." Faith clutched her right arm. It was sore and felt like a Charley horse.

It was Gabe.

It's Gabe! It's not one of the doctors coming to ask me the same questions again, Faith thought in relief.

"Hey, Faith, I wanted to drop by. I hope you don't mind," Gabe said.

"No, that's okay," Faith said. *You can come any time you like.*

"Hey, Gabe," Mom said.

"Hey, Mrs. Amber," Gabe echoed.

Gabe glanced down and noticed that Faith was holding her arm. She also rubbed her foot.

"Well, I was coming from my auntie's house that's around here. I picked up a card for you. I would've made one for you and printed it out, but we were out of ink. We picked the card up on the way to my aunt's, but...." Gabe sat on her bed. "I'll let you open it."

"Oh, you mean one of your mom's close friends? You always call your mom's besties 'auntie,'" Faith chuckled as she looked up at him. "You didn't have to get me anything."

"You always say that," Gabe said as Faith ripped open the envelope and tore the golden circle sticker.

"I'm sorry about ruining the envelope. I can't open it carefully," Faith apologized.

"Oh, it's okay," Gabe said. "Don't worry about the envelope."

"Can you read it for me? As you know, I can't because of my CVI. I need my big 48 print. It needs to be magenta, backlit, and have a bright yellow background. Thanks to my handy-dandy iPad, I can actually see to read—thank goodness!" Faith grinned and extended the envelope to Gabe. She suppressed laughter and pressed her head against her propped-up pillows. "Excuse my appearance. I look like half a mummy. They always wrap my head in gauze to keep the electrodes in place."

"That's all right, Faith, I don't care. I came to see your mom —not you. Hi, Mrs. Amber—*again*!" Faith and Gabe burst out laughing.

"I'm going to stretch my legs," Mom said and left the room.

The card was of a blue and green sky. Depicted on the front were dandelions and fluffy seeds flying away. It had blue shiny-reflective cursive.

Gabe read, "It says on the front: 'The Lord's love never ends; His mercies never stop. They are new every morning. Lamentations 3:22, 23.'"

With her arms under her head, Faith said pensively, "That's nice."

"It is nice," Gabe said as he glanced on the inside.

"Do you like to read the Bible?" Faith asked, staring up at the ceiling.

"Well, I like some verses. I do read the daily readings, but I don't like to read the Bible in its full form. I mean, I don't read the whole Bible, book by book in its entirety for fun," Gabe explained as he tapped his finger on his chin.

"I really like the Gospels, and the Old Testament—mostly about Abraham and Sarah. I always read Bishop Robert Baron's daily Gospel reflections and the daily readings just like you do," Faith commented. There was a hesitation. "What does it say on the inside of the card?" she asked.

Gabe read as he glanced at her, saying, "'Just a little reminder that you are in God's care and in my prayers today.' Here," he handed her a gift bag.

"I love it. It's so sweet. I like the greeting," Faith said and gave Gabe a grateful look.

"Ooh, pretty bag!" Faith cried as Gabe smiled, his white teeth glistening. "Let's see." She pulled back the hot pink tissue paper that was sticking out of the bag. "Ooh! Pretty! Hershey's dark chocolate! Extra-large! That was very considerate." She held up the chocolate bar. "Want to share it?"

"Nah, it's yours," Gabe declined with a shooing motion of his hand. He stuffed his hand in his pocket.

"Okay. Are you sure before I dig into it?" Faith offered.

"Sure—I'm more of a cookie kind of guy," Gabe said and Faith sanitized her hands. She broke off a piece, and Gabe took it anyway. "But I'll join in to share the joy."

"Mmm," Faith said.

"You know, this tastes like vanilla-flavored sanitizer now," Gabe said as he looked at the bright light above Faith's bed.

"I'm sorry. I just wanted to sanitize.... Never mind." She hesitated. "Sorry, I have to use the restroom. I need to unplug the finger wrap and heart monitor. Where's that thing?" Faith's fingers searched for the plug. She slugged the blue Velcro bag over her shoulder, which held the box that had the colorful wires that were attached to Faith's electrodes. She threw back the heavy blankets and searched for the receptacle where all the wires were attached.

"Here, I'll help you," Gabe said as he fumbled with the plug.

"Mom, can you help me?" Faith asked as Mom appeared in the doorway.

"Got it?" Gabe asked as the blue bag slid down her shoulder.

"When is Dad coming?" Faith asked.

"In about twenty minutes," Mom said as she helped.

"I need to get that IV cord," Faith said. Her legs wobbled. "I haven't exercised—being in bed for three days really takes a toll on me."

When she returned from the bathroom, Faith got under the covers again.

Gabe sighed. "Lots of paraphernalia you have to schlep."

"It's not too bad. I'm used to it. That card was sweet—I really like it. Can you set it next to the pretty tulips you gave me? They're beside the TV on that shelf attached to the wall. I love the brightness and color of the flowers," Faith said softly.

"Is that good?" Gabe asked and turned to her. The warm golden light gave a luster to his cream-colored hair. His hair was in its usual, perpetually orderly state.

"Yeah, it's good," Faith smiled.

After Gabe left, Faith began to write in her journal. When dinner arrived, she heard another knock.

"Hey, Faith," a youth said.

"Caleb," smiled Faith. She laughed softly.

"How is my Faith doing today?" grinned Caleb. "Sorry about my sweaty clothes. I just came from basketball practice." He smiled playfully at Faith. It always seemed to brighten her spirits. He leaned over to hug her and she made a face as she scanned his body, which was damp with perspiration.

"I'm just teasing. I know I'm super gross right now," Caleb said jokingly.

"How are you?" Faith inquired.

"The boys and I went to get pizza. Speaking of which, I got you three slices. I know how much you hate to eat, so I only got you three." Caleb cracked up at his own joke.

"As I always say, I eat to live, but I don't live to eat," laughed Faith. "I'll stick them in the mini fridge for my piggy dad. I'll eat one—he'll eat the other two."

"I love to eat, but I don't live to eat. I love sweets," Caleb chuckled.

"You guys are spoiling me," laughed Faith as she played with the corners of her pillow.

"Has Grace called?" Caleb asked.

"No, but I plan to call her," Faith said. "Would you like to share the second half of my sandwich? There's no way I could eat the rest," Faith said generously.

"Sure, I love sandwiches." Caleb reached over. He bit into the turkey sandwich. Faith gave him a napkin.

"Want to watch a movie?"

"Sure! What do you want to watch? They've got movies here? Oh, you got flowers! They're so colorful! Who got them for you?" Caleb asked as he lay on his stomach on the edge of her hospital bed.

"Gabe," blushed Faith, her cheeks heating up. She hid a smile in vain. Faith wasn't sure that Gabe had any romantic interest in her, and she knew that she shouldn't get her hopes up.

"Gabe's really nice to you. He loves you a lot, you know that?" Caleb remarked as he smiled knowingly and looked down at his sandwich. Faith shrugged sheepishly.

After Caleb left, Faith's phone indicated a text. It was from Tracy.

Tracy: So, Gabe's concert is coming up. I wonder if I could come with you guys?

Faith: Oh, sure. You can join in.

Tracy: Okay, great! I can't wait.

Faith: Me neither!

An hour later, Faith called Grace.

"Hi, Grace, how are you?" Faith asked.

"I'm good—you?" Grace answered.

"I'm well," Faith replied. "What have you been up to?"

"Schoolwork. My brain is tired," Grace said. Faith laughed.

"So, Tracy wants to come to Gabe's concert. Is that okay with you?" Faith asked. "The more the merrier, right?"

"Oh yeah, sure, the more the merrier.... What have you been up to?" Grace inquired absently.

"Well, I wrote in my journal, read lots of cool books for school, and wrote some essay answers. Nurses and doctors have been in and out," Faith responded. "Gabe visited today."

"Again? Why? It's a long drive from his house," Grace said, perplexed.

"Well, he said he was going to visit his mom's friend who lives nearby the hospital. What's her name?" Faith continued.

"What friend?" asked Grace confusedly.

"I don't know," said Faith, shrugging. "Gabe said he was visiting one of his aunties."

"We have no auntie who lives near there," Grace said.

"Oh..." Faith said as she hugged the card to her chest. She picked up her candy bar and bit into it as she gazed at her tulips.

Chapter Thirteen

"Hey, can I come in?" Tracy asked as she tapped on the door. She poked her head into the room.

"Tracy! You came!" Faith exclaimed.

"I didn't bring anything. I just rushed over." Tracy flopped her hands on her thighs.

"You're giving me your time," Faith said.

"Yeah...um...I just wanna say...I'm sorry I treated you badly. You don't deserve that; you've always treated me nicely.... I hope you can forgive me." Tracy looked down and bit on her bottom lip as she sat on the edge of Faith's bed. Faith opened her mouth to say something, and realized Tracy wasn't done. "I don't have friends."

"What do you mean?" Faith asked.

"I mean, I've had plenty of people who I *thought* were my friends."
Faith gave her a concerned look.

"I've known so much rejection, I'm afraid all of my relationships will fall apart," Tracy said.

"Well, you only need one good friend, and maybe God doesn't want those people in your life. Some people just aren't worth it...."

"Huh. I never thought of it like that before. In my experience, relationships don't last long," Tracy said.

"No?"

"I've had great experiences with friends in the past, but not in the last few years. My mom and dad say to be myself and to be kind to everyone, which I really try to be. I know I can be negative a lot—I don't mean to be. I get so down, anxious, and frustrated! So, that's another reason why making friends can be a struggle. But I can be happy just like any other person. When I finally think I actually made a real friend, they leave me hanging by saying they're busy, or they say they'd like to talk to me, but they make excuses why they can't.

"I understand that people can be busy, but it happens too often for me to believe it anymore. I think I'd be a millionaire if I got a dollar every time I've been put off, ghosted, and left hanging. It feels like usually a one-sided relationship, because I'm always the one reaching out. Guys don't even talk to me, and girls can get cliquey. It's dehumanizing to me. I've got feelings, too.

"But then I feel like maybe I'm not likable or something—I know I can be mean sometimes. I don't want to be that way. I always wind up alone, which is fine, because I don't mind being alone. I'm more an introvert, anyway. Friendships are overrated. But with you—you have a lot of friends. You're so sweet, honest, pretty, and talented," Tracy said hesitantly, reddening. "You're not afraid to be yourself—no matter what."

Faith glanced down at her hands and blushed.

"You are," Tracy said.

"Thank you." Faith smiled as a short hesitation ensued.

"Actually, to be totally honest, you're not looking so special right now," Tracy said teasingly with a laugh. Faith and Tracy burst out laughing together.

"Anyway, I was jealous of you. I'm sorry—I truly am," Tracy said.

"You're forgiven," Faith said and smiled. She squeezed Tracy's hand. "It'll be okay. You can always text or call if you need to talk," Faith smiled.

"Thanks, Faith," Tracy remarked. "I have such bad anxiety. I feel like something bad is going to happen all the time, and I'm always worried. Most days, I cry when I get home from school, and I feel down and worthless. I feel cranky most of the time, and nothing gives me joy like it used to when I was younger. I can't seem to sleep at night. I'm doing a monologue here. I can't believe I'm telling you all this. It must be boring you."

"No, no. I'm glad you felt like you could tell me," Faith said. "All of that sounds really hard."

"It is…but I've said enough," Tracy said.

"What are you doing today?" Faith asked, changing the subject.

"Well, tonight, Mom and I are going to see a horror movie at the theater," Tracy explained with a shrug.

"Do you like horror movies?" Faith inquired.

"I love them—I like the thrill."

"What else do you like?"

"As I said at the restaurant, I'm obsessed with breakup songs. I like to belt them out in my room," Tracy laughed. "Speaking of exciting things coming up…" Tracy made a half-smile. "I can't wait for Gabe's concert. It's going to be so fun."

"Yeah, can't wait," Faith said.

Tracy's bright red lips formed into a small smile. "Faith, what do you do while you're stuck here? It's a good thing that you don't have to do school."

"I do, actually. I'm still reading classics, doing math, and continuing to study science. Mom and I are reading Scripture and discussing it every day."

"My parents and I don't read Scripture or go to church. My parents gave up on it when they were young. The only reason they send me to Catholic school is because of the discipline." She laughed. "They think I need it…. God and I were never close."

"You can still get close to God. I once read a good book called *Motorcycles, Sushi, and One Strange Book* by Nancy Rue. I think you'd like it; here, you can write it down—there's a notepad and a pencil in the hospital tray." Tracy got out the pad and pencil from the tray and she scribbled the title and the author on the yellow paper.

"Thanks," Tracy said, her face serious again.

The nurse came in to replace the electrodes, and Tracy thought it was a good time to say goodbye.

* * *

"What happened to your temples?" Grace asked Faith as the three girls walked toward the school auditorium. Tracy had joined Faith and Grace for Gabe's choir concert. It was a cold, late autumn evening. The sun had set with a pink and gold streak, and it was getting dark.

"The glue that the nurses put on my electrodes burned my skin and left scabs."

Grace pulled Faith aside, saying, "Why is Tracy here?"

"I...I invited her," Faith replied softly. She felt her cheeks get hot.

"Why? Why do you keep inviting her?" Grace looked angry. She took Faith by the shoulders.

"I already asked you when I called you from the hospital..." was the reply.

"My mind was on the periodic table," Grace said. "That doesn't count."

"Yes, it does. She wants to see Gabe sing just like we do," Faith said calmly. Despite this, her heart was beating rapidly and her stomach began to get upset.

Grace stalked away toward the open doors of the school building.

"What's up with her?" Tracy asked as she and Faith entered the auditorium and sat down. Immediately, Tracy got back up and walked toward the vending machine, as Grace headed toward the bathroom.

"Excuse me, pardon me." Caleb appeared in the row. He walked sideways as the people in the aisle pulled their knees in.

"Hey, Caleb," Faith said glumly as she crossed her arms.

"What's up, Faith?" Caleb asked.

"Grace is overwhelmed about Tracy. I should probably talk to her." Faith blew air through her lips as she slumped in her seat.

"Nah, leave her alone. She'll cool off soon enough," Caleb said as he sat down beside her.

"Grace is upset because I invited Tracy. She claims her mind was on science and school when I asked her on the phone." Faith buried her head in her hands.

"How is it up to Grace who you invite?" Caleb asked as he turned to look her square in the eye.

"I don't know—I know that Grace doesn't like her," Faith shrugged.

"I don't see how that's your problem. Seems more like it's Grace's problem. Let's just focus on Gabe's singing for now. You can talk to her after," Caleb remarked.

"Yeah," Faith said and exhaled deeply. She noticed Caleb look over her head, and smile broadly. She turned to look and saw Bethany standing in the aisle.

During his solo, Gabe passionately sang on the stage. His polyester blue robe glittered in the light. Faith craned her neck to try to get a better view of Gabe, but the guy in front of her seemed to have an un-usually large head.

* * *

After the show, Gabe trotted down the long, purple, and blue tile hallway toward Faith.

"What did you think?" Gabe asked, grinning.

"It was great." Faith looked down at her sturdy leather heels.

"You don't sound sincere." Gabe's shoulders sagged. "What's up?"

"It wasn't your singing. That's not why I'm on edge," Faith gestured to herself with her fingertips.

Gabe leaned closer to her ear. "Is it you and Tracy?"

Shaking her head, Faith remarked, "No, Tracy and I are fine. We made up."

"When did that happen?" Gabe asked.

"A couple of days ago at the hospital," Faith answered.

"Then is it you and Grace?" inquired Gabe.

"Yes," Faith said. "She claims her mind was on school when I asked if Tracy could come to your concert. Caleb said it's not my problem."

"Ohh!" Gabe stuffed his hands in his pockets. He swayed back and forth as he looked up at the ceiling. He blew air through his lips, and it came out like a whistle. "For the first time, I actually agree with Caleb on something substantial! Not your problem!"

"I shouldn't be talking about this right now. I thought you did excellently. You're really talented," Faith complimented. She glanced at Grace, who was scrolling through her phone over by the trophy cases.

"I can't do anything to help you except break the ice and be there," Gabe said, looking at the wall.

"Thank you.... Wait, no! I don't want you to be in that position. I know what that's like. It wipes one out. I've been there when I was trying to be the peacemaker with Tracy and Grace," Faith said quietly.

"Hey, Grace." Gabe offered a smile.

Grace looked annoyed and then said, "Good job." She looked over at Faith.

"I can't believe you invited Tracy to this. I feel like we're drifting apart," Grace said dramatically.

"No, we're not. I don't love you any less than I ever did. We have enough love in our hearts for many people. I love you all—I love all my friends," Faith explained. Coming from the bathroom, Tracy and Bethany walked up from behind Faith.

"Why do you keep inviting her to everything?" Grace cried and walked into the girls' bathroom. Faith looked at Tracy as she smiled sympathetically and set a hand reassuringly on Tracy's arm. Bethany exchanged a worried glance with Faith.

Faith turned to Gabe, shrugging. "I tried."

* * *

Faith lay on her bed and thought about the day: Grace was especially cold toward Tracy and Faith. Caleb was quite comical and his normal, boisterous self. Poor Gabe conversed normally; he was in a feigned happy mood—smiling and talking. Tracy said nothing most of the time. But when she did, she spoke with Caleb. It was a little confusing to Faith to decide whether to sign the lyrics for Bethany at Gabe's concert.

Faith heard her phone ring. It was Gabe!

"How are you? I hope I helped despite my awkwardness. I hope everything turns out okay."

"Thank you so much for being there for me," Faith smiled.

"You're welcome! Well...I've got to go. I just thought I'd call and let you know you were on my mind," Gabe said.

"Oh! All right, okay then. Um, bye!" Faith said.

Wow! That was nice of him to call and say that I was on his mind, but it was odd since that was, like, a ten-second call.

Faith's phone rang and she jumped. Tracy's name popped up on the screen.

Faith picked up.

"I'm sorry I made it hard for you, Faith. I made it hard for all of you. I know Grace doesn't like me. You don't have to invite me to anything anymore."

"I *want* to invite you. Who cares what Grace thinks?" Faith remarked. *Oh my goodness! I really feel that way.*

"Really?" Tracy asked quietly.

"Yeah, it's Grace's problem. She'll get over it," Faith said.

The girls said their goodbyes.

* * *

The next day, Faith was reading articles for school on her bed. She was still upset about Grace, but she was trying to push past it.

Faith's phone rang.

Grace began immediately, "I'm sorry for being icy toward you and Tracy. I'm really sorry. I was being such a baby. You've been my best friend forever—I just don't like, um...want to lose you, you know?"

Relief washed over Faith.

Faith closed her eyes and sincerely said, "I forgive you."

* * *

Bethany and Caleb ran with their arms shielding their heads, laughing. Rain pelted on the asphalt parking lot, leaving puddles everywhere. In front of Mr. Xiao's music store a teal wooden sign swung above the music store's door and it said in white: *Bethany Xiao's Jams*.

"Hey, Dad," Bethany smiled, signing.

"Who's this?" Mr. Xiao asked, signing. "Caleb? Your boyfriend?"

"No," Bethany laughed softly.

"You just got back from the dance studio, huh?" asked Mr. Xiao.

"Yeah, Caleb met Mom and me there," Bethany explained. "How are the sales?"

"They're doing well—it's a little slow today, probably because of the rain," Mr. Xiao replied, signing. "What is your favorite instrument, little buddy?" inquired Mr. Xiao, signing and speaking at the same time.

"Dad! Please," Bethany blushed.

"No offense taken," Caleb said. "I like drums and my acoustic guitar. I always wanted a red, shiny rock guitar and an amp when I was little." Mr. Xiao translated for Bethany.

"We have those two things here," Bethany remarked.

"Feel free to wander around, Caleb, and check out all the instruments," Mr. Xiao said to Caleb, signing simultaneously. Caleb raised a hand and walked off with a grin.

"Score!" Mr. Xiao jabbed Bethany in the ribs.

"Ow! Dad, he's just a good friend," Bethany signed. She played with a silver button on her light denim jacket.

Moments later, Mr. Xiao took his daughter by the hand and led her to the percussion department where Caleb was playing the drums with headphones on.

"He's my kinda guy. You know, I enjoyed rockin' out on the drums when I was his age," Mr. Xiao signed to Bethany.

"You really like playing the drums," Bethany signed to Caleb. Caleb gave a thumbs-up.

"I love 'em, too. I drove Grandma Xiao nuts," laughed Mr. Xiao.

"My mom's the same way," chuckled Caleb. "Right on, dude...I mean, Mr. Xiao." Caleb fist-bumped Mr. Xiao.

"I like your little boyfriend," Mr. Xiao signed, and patted his daughter on the shoulder.

"Dad! He's not my little boyfriend," Bethany signed, growling.

Caleb was too involved in playing the drums to see the exchange. He picked up his backpack from the floor and got out his phone.

"Did you read the scriptural readings today? Mark 7:31-37?" asked Caleb energetically.

Mr. Xiao translated for Bethany. "I'll let you two just text. I've got a customer."

"Okay," Bethany replied in sign to her dad. She turned to Caleb. "Oh, the one about Jesus healing the blind-deaf man?" Bethany asked, texting on her phone. "I like that one. I always thought it was gross because Jesus put His spit on the deaf man's tongue."

Caleb burst out laughing. "Bethany, He spit on the ground and touched his tongue."

"Really? I'm pretty sure He spit *on* his tongue," chuckled Bethany, texting.

"Let's look it up," Caleb suggested. "I was right. Jesus touched his tongue and spat on the ground..."

Bethany laughed. "Wow! I was way off. What an amazing miracle. Through Jesus, anything is possible."

"What is your favorite Scripture?" Caleb asked.

"Psalm 30:12: 'You changed my mourning into dancing; you took off my sackcloth and clothed me with gladness.' I love the meaning of it. Whenever I'm sad, I can read it and feel better," Bethany sighed contently.

"Are you involved in a Bible study?" Caleb asked.

"All the parishioners who are deaf at my church get together every Thursday night for Bible study. Did you know I have a gig at the theater?" Bethany smiled. "Want to come?"

* * *

Caleb stood in the doorway of the downtown theater as he spoke to a security guard.

"Can you give these flowers to Bethany Xiao? She's my friend. Tell her they're from uh...like, Caleb," Caleb said as he handed them to a security guard.

"Yes, sir," the burly security man said. He wore a headset and a black t-shirt, and his dreadlocks were pulled back in a ponytail.

"You came!" Faith exclaimed in surprise. "Such a lovely bouquet. She's gonna love them," Faith smiled. "Let's go inside."

"Too bad the other guys couldn't join up with us," Caleb remarked.

"Yeah, they're going to the next performance," Faith replied.

"Be careful not to step on anyone," Caleb said as they made their way through the crowd. There was a loud hubbub of laughter and chatting. It was apparent that the huge crowd was excited to hear the music and see Bethany's talent.

"I'll use you as a service dog," Faith joked. Caleb laughed as she took his arm.

The two friends went down the burgundy-carpeted aisle that had golden floral print. The large, elaborate stage had a golden awning. They took their seats as the lights dimmed. As the gold-embroidered, red curtain rose, a young male dancer and Bethany began dancing. A grand instrumental ballad of "Once Upon a Dream" was played by a magnificent orchestra. Faith watched the elderly conductor move his arms gracefully, as beautiful music came out of the violins. Caleb tapped his feet and kept in time with the music.

"Beautiful, and Bethany looks like an elegant princess," Faith whispered into Caleb's ear.

"I know," Caleb whispered back as he watched, amazed, as the two dancers glided across the floor. "I think she's gorgeous."

* * *

Bethany had given permission for Caleb and Faith to join her backstage, as she already knew they were coming.

Caleb and Faith maneuvered through the crowd and were guided backstage by a security guard. Leading the two friends, the security guard dropped them off at Bethany's dressing room door. Caleb knocked.

"Hi, Caleb," Bethany signed with a bright expression.

"It was amazing," Caleb breathed.

"Thanks," Bethany signed with a modest expression.

"You looked like a graceful princess," Faith added as she signed. "Like Aurora."

"That's what the makeup artists were aiming for," Bethany said. "Sorry if my makeup is overwhelming—the artists wanted the audience to see my face clearly."

"You look nice," Caleb smiled. "Even in stage makeup."

"My hair's crazy and I feel really hot," laughed Bethany. "I'm sweaty. I'm doing the same show again in ninety minutes. Thanks for the bouquet."

Caleb chuckled, saying, "I don't know how you feel about dyed daisies, though."

"I love them. So pretty," Bethany signed as she glanced over at them on her dressing table.

Faith was translating for Caleb. "Hey, I actually got some of the signing! Wanna get some Swedish fish out of the vending machine?" asked Caleb.

"There's a lounge here that's only for the performers. They'll have junk food, but no Swedish fish," Bethany signed.

"I'm down for that."

"I'll wait here for a minute," Faith smiled knowingly. "You guys can text each other."

"No, you can come," Bethany said in sign language.

"No, Caleb can have a break from being my service dog. I'll wait here." Faith settled herself on the couch.

Caleb and Bethany went down several tiled hallways into a kitchen with a coffeemaker, a sink, a silver fridge, and a round table.

Caleb took his phone out of his back pocket and Bethany, smiling, got out hers. They sat down at the table and began to text.

Bethany: I can't be too long because I've gotta shower and go into hair and makeup.

Caleb: Okay, I got you. I just wanted to show you this real quick. Look what I found: 1 Corinthians 13:4-8.

Bethany: You are a whiz with Scripture.

Caleb got a package of Skittles out of his back pocket.

Bethany: Let me search it on my phone.

Caleb began to read. "1 Corinthians…13:4-8. Ah, here it is: 'Love is patient, love is kind. It is not jealous, [love] is not pompous, it is not inflated, it is not rude, it does not seek its own interests, it is not quick-tempered, it does not brood over injury, it does not rejoice over wrong-doing but rejoices with the truth. It bears all things, believes all things, hopes all things, endures all things. Love never fails,'" Caleb read slowly, then pondered about it for a moment.

Bethany was reading the scriptural passage and was nodding.

Bethany: It's like a true guide to what true love is, isn't it?

Bethany tilted her head. Her brown eyes were full of laughter and hope—like they always were.

Caleb: Yeah.

He half-smiled.

Caleb: So, I was wondering if we could go to Steak 'n Shake sometime?

Bethany: Yeah, I'd like that.

She smiled.

* * *

"Faith, you're not going to believe this," Bethany signed after she closed her dressing room door. "Caleb asked me out."

"Yay!" Faith sprang up and shouted with joy.

"Never have I been asked out in my entire life!" Bethany's eyes shone in the lamplight.

"Speaking of Caleb, where is he?" Faith asked.

"He's searching for a vending machine," Bethany said. "He'll meet you in a minute."

The girls talked for a moment, and then Bethany had to go shower and get ready again.

* * *

Gabe heard his phone ring and saw that it was Faith. His heart leaped and a smile formed on his lips.

Gabe answered.

"Um...Gabe?"

"Yes, Faith," Gabe said. *Is she sick?*

"The...the doctor called and said they have an opening for the brain surgery to be performed," Faith explained timidly.

"Wow, I thought it'd be a year from now," Gabe answered. "When is it?"

Faith hesitated. "On opening night..."

"Ohh," Gabe replied and rubbed his eyes. "Let's FaceTime. It's easier for you to understand what I'm saying when my facial expressions are added." They disconnected and reconnected on FaceTime.

"Dr. Philips said I have to take this spot, because the brain surgeon is booked for the whole year," Faith continued in almost a whisper.

"I feel so much anxiety in my chest right now. I don't want anything bad to happen to you, but I want you to feel better," Gabe commented. "I—I know. You can't live like this anymore because you're miserable every day," Gabe managed to get out—a lump forming in his throat. "I'll come over! Hold on!"

* * *

Gabe sat down on the dark blue couch as he rubbed his hands together. Although the sunlight streamed through the living room's wide window, it didn't help Gabe's mood.

"One time I heard this one thing, Faith, that a person could feel more than one feeling at a time. You know?"

Faith gave him a weak smile and a shrug.

"You could die, you know?" Gabe's voice was firm.

"My doctor never said that. You're exaggerating." Faith put her hands on her hips.

"But then there's worse stuff than death. As you told me, there're other risks—like infection...migraines, or brain bleed. Brain bleeds are just like a stroke! I thought your doctor said you couldn't have it because it was too risky? Don't they need to know exactly where the damaged spot is, or else they'll just be putting electrodes in your brain? What if it's not successful, and then they'll just be digging in your brain and drilling those holes for nothing? Those are holes in your *skull*!"

Faith was silent for a moment and said, "I mean, what if they *do* find something? What if they find where the seizures are originating, and they can take it out? What if none of those risks happen? I could be healed," Faith said with emphasis as she paced back and forth. She stopped in front of her friend. "Gabe, this is a huge opportunity. If I don't take it, I'll have to wait a whole 'nother year for this. What happens if I don't go through with this and feel seizure sick for the big stuff? You know—my wedding day, the birth of my children, and all the times you're supposed to enjoy?"

"Nobody enjoys childbirth," Gabe shook his head. "If you did, you'd be weird."

Faith ignored Gabe's attempt at humor. "Right now, truthfully, I can't even enjoy watching fun movies, talking to my friends, or going to parties. I have to force past sickness!"

"I know, but I don't want you to suffer from migraines or come out of the surgery as someone completely different. What if your memory gets erased? All our precious memories would be gone. Those are important!" replied Gabe vehemently.

"You sound like my mom right now. She doesn't want me to have it either, because she's worried. Ye of little faith!" Faith shouted.

"Don't use Scripture against me!" Gabe said impulsively.

"Gabe, I thought you wanted me to have this. But right now...you don't sound like it." Faith looked down, hurt. After a short hesitation, she looked up, determined, her light red eyebrows furrowing. "I want to enjoy little things *and* the big things."

"Can't you already?" Gabe asked.

"Yes. But not to the extent I could if I weren't sick," Faith replied quickly. "Gabe?" Tears ran down Faith's cheeks. "Why don't you get this?"

Gabe was choking up as he said softly, "Faith, you don't understand. I want you to have it, but...I'm—I'm too scared."

"Why don't you get it?" Faith repeated, tears forming in her beautiful brown eyes. Gabe leaned toward her and started to open his arms. Faith thought he was going to hug her. Then his arms fell down at his sides. Gabe looked deeply into her brown eyes that were usually so gentle and full of wonder. But not now. They were full of indignation and anguish.

"I do, Faith, but you're my best friend..." Gabe said. "You make me laugh like nobody else...I feel extremely comfortable around you. You make me really...I can't really explain it. I don't want you to be taken away from me."

A few uncomfortable minutes had passed, and Gabe and Faith were still in the living room. Gabe was playing with the laces of his sneakers. There was an awkward silence in the room.

I want to feel better more than anything. I would take the risk of dying or worse things. That want is stronger than anything. If I don't take the chance, I'll feel miserable. I can't bear that idea.

Faith could understand why Gabe wouldn't want her to have the surgery, but why was he so strong about it? Why did he have to persist? Faith thought he would say, "Go for it! I'll be with you all the way." But no…. She couldn't understand it. She glanced at him out of the corner of her eye. He looked upset, too, but continued to ignore her.

"I'll be praying for you, and I'll call you later," Gabe said as he stood up and walked out of the house.

Once he was on the front porch and had closed the door, Gabe whispered to himself, "And…I love you."

Chapter Fourteen

Faith heard the garage door open and close. "Hey, Faith, I'm home from work," Dad said as he sat down in his armchair. "What's wrong?" He noted the tears on his daughter's cheeks.

"Gabe is scared that something bad will happen to me if I have surgery. I thought he would be more supportive," Faith said, sitting down as she buried her head in her hands.

"But honey...I'm sure he loves you—he's probably worried just like the rest of us," Dad said.

"Who loves whom?" Mom asked, her bright red hair in a clip.

Faith burst into tears. She flopped her hands on her thighs. "I love him, Mom..." Mom put her arm around her daughter as she cried.

Faith sniffled as Mom said, "I know, honey."

* * *

Meanwhile, Gabe was in his bedroom on his bed talking to his mom.

"I wouldn't be able to bear it, Mom. I don't want her to suffer," Gabe said. He pinched his nose.

"It's a miscommunication, honey," Mrs. Charles said.

"I don't know what to do.... Should I go over? Should I call her?"

"Give it a couple hours, sweetheart," Mrs. Charles said. "But she's been sick since kindergarten. She needs this—put yourself in her shoes. I'm sure the surgeons wouldn't attempt something so invasive if they thought it wouldn't help her."

"I hate to see her so upset," Gabe said. "I need to talk to her.... Opening night is tomorrow evening. She's supposed to have the surgery tomorrow," Gabe said as he stood up.

"I know, sweetie. Faith makes you so happy. I can see it on your face and hear it when you're laughing on the phone," Mrs. Charles said.

* * *

Later that afternoon, Faith knocked on Gabe's front door and waited. She glanced toward her mom, who was sitting in the running car.

"Hi, Faith," Gabe said as he opened the shiny oak door and walked out onto the gray stone porch. The navy-painted house had a patio and wicker furniture under the veranda. "I got your text that you were coming."

Gabe glanced briefly at Faith and then looked down.

"I just wanted to do a drop-off." Faith looked fixedly down at the manila envelope in her hands. "I want you to read this after my surgery.... I have to go now." She started to walk toward the car.

"Wait, Faith!" Faith waited expectantly. "Goodbye! Good luck," Gabe said as Faith got into the car and drove away. He looked down at the heavy envelope.

* * *

A large crowd of Costco customers rushed into the spacious warehouse at ten o'clock. Their voices echoed throughout the aisles.

"What flowers would you like?" Mrs. Charles asked.

"Mom! It's almost time for her surgery. What do you think?" Gabe asked, looking at his phone.

"What about these carnations?" suggested Mrs. Charles.

"She likes roses or those bright blue and dark pink daisies," Gabe said.

"What about these light pink roses?" Mrs. Charles asked as she picked up the bouquet. She studied her son's face closely. "You look terrified."

"I know…I don't want to lose her. She might not come back.… She might…die," Gabe worried as he tapped his foot quickly.

"We'll buy these," Mrs. Charles stated as she got a bag for the flowers. "As it says in Matthew 6:34: 'Do not worry about tomorrow; tomorrow will take care of itself.' Oh no," Mrs. Charles said as she looked at the check-out registers. "There's a very long line."

"We can't wait!" Gabe cried.

"We've got plenty of time, sweetheart," reassured Mrs. Charles.

Lying in bed, wearing her stained work smock, Mary looked up at her ceiling. Now was the time. Focusing on each floorboard, she carefully stepped over the creaky ones and headed toward the door. Creak.... She waited, sweat beading down her forehead as she tried to steady her breathing. Her heart was in her throat and she felt like she was going to retch.

Slipping out the front door and across the pasture, Mary bolted toward the forest. She entered the opening of the trees and looked around. At first, all she could see was blackness. But then she saw Mark's tall figure approach her, twigs crunching beneath his feet.

"It's okay," Mark whispered as he held her arm and guided her forward. They walked past various towering trees, underbrush, streams, and ponds. They then entered the empty city, framed by lofty brick buildings.

"I'm so frightened, Mark," Mary said as they approached the railway station with its stone walkway, canopy, and pillars. "But I know we must do this." She looked at him with anxious eyes, as he put his arm around her. Mary's legs were tired while Mark led her along. She wrapped her arms around herself because of the chill, and Mark offered his blazer to her.

In the dead of night, the railway station was desolate, except for the single shabby-looking man who was loading the cargo with burdensome wooden crates. The railway station was pitch black except for the moonlight and the twinkling of the stars above.

Surveying the area around him, Mark spotted a stack of the massive wooden crates that might shield them from the cargo-loading man.

"Hide behind these boxes. We don't have the money for a ticket. We'll have to conceal ourselves in one of the boxcars," said Mark as he took her hand and they stood behind a large wooden crate.

"Are you certain this is safe?" Mary whispered, her soft, small, trembling hand in his.

"Indeed...trust me," Mark said as he looked at her steadily with such wisdom and love. He surveyed the surroundings before putting his hands around Mary's narrow waist, and he lifted her inside the boxcar. He climbed in beside her and they hid in the farthest corner behind a row of wooden crates. They slid onto their knees and sighed with relief.

Mary buried her face into the handkerchief that Mother had given her and cried. She closed her eyes and let tears of relief stream down her face. Mark's eyes glistened with tears as he sniffled. The two of them remained quiet. Mary felt safe in Mark's presence, although she heard the heavy footfall of a man outside the metal door of the boxcar. They peered out from their hiding place, their hearts hammering against their ribcages and sweat forming on their upper lips, as the gruff man closed the front door of the boxcar with a clang.

They were now cast into complete darkness. Their eyes began to adjust to the blackness. Mary and Mark felt the floor of the boxcar shake as the train started to move. Mark squeezed Mary's hand and brushed loose strands of her black hair away from her forehead as he gazed at her tenderly. Mark kissed her gently on the lips as they stayed in the corner, hushed.

After Faith changed into her hospital gown, got her heart monitor, and got into bed, Mom and Dad exited the room and walked down the hall. Tears rolled down Mom's cheeks as Dad held her, stroking her hair.

"There's so much at stake—I'm still frightened," Mom said softly.

"It's okay, Amber," soothed Dad. "God is looking out for us. This could be the healing we've been praying for."

* * *

Mrs. Charles had just parked the van in a parking spot as Gabe looked down at the rose bouquet in his lap. Gabe rushed ahead of his mother through the hospital doors toward the elevators.

"Hold that door!" Gabe said as one of the elevators' doors started to close. Red numbers flashed on the screen in the elevator while Gabe watched with restlessness as people exited.

"It's taking forever!" Gabe groaned. "We've got to hurry!"

"I'll be in the waiting room," said Mrs. Charles.

"Great, Mom," Gabe said absently.

Wonderful! All these halls look the same, Gabe thought as he made circles through the endless corridors. He finally found the nurses' desk.

After asking where Faith's room was, the nurse explained, "She's about to go into surgery.... I think she's just waiting for a nurse to take her to the operating room." She pointed to the correct hallway with her pen.

"Thank you," Gabe said as he walked hurriedly down the hall. He desperately wanted to run, but he didn't want to collide into people. His heart beat rapidly.

Gabe quickly skimmed the room numbers and the signs. He licked his sweaty upper lip and wiped it with his black jacket sleeve.

560, 561, 562...564! At last! This is it! He noticed Faith's parents hugging each other in the doorframe.

"Gabe?" Mom asked, surprised.

"Hi, Mrs. Amber, Mr. Daniel," Gabe said as he rushed into the room.

"You came in the nick of time. The nurse is going to start her IV," Mom remarked.

"Gabe...you came?" Faith asked.

Faith lay on a wide and rigid hospital bed surrounded by monitors and IV bags. It was clear from the large window that it was still misty outside from the early morning.

"I had to see you before you went into the operating room," Gabe said.

"You look like you just ran a marathon. Are you okay? You look exhausted," Faith observed.

Gabe panted, "I read your manuscript—I couldn't wait. It's fantastic!" He bent over and put his hands on his knees. He sat down on the edge of her bed.

"You *did*? It *is*?" Faith asked. "I didn't know it was any good."

"It's totally awesome. Faith...God gave you the gift of writing," Gabe told her.

"He did?" Faith asked, utterly baffled.

"Yes. It's deep, detailed, and emotional," smiled Gabe. A short pause ensued. "So...is this Mark guy based on me?"

Blushing, Faith shrugged, saying, "Kinda." She smiled sheepishly.

A hurried nurse poked her head into the room. "I was going to start her IV, but I can come back in a few minutes," she said with understanding, as she glanced from Faith to Gabe. "Is this your boyfriend?"

"Kinda," Gabe answered.

Faith grinned in spite of herself.

"We should say a prayer," Gabe remarked.

"You're right," Faith agreed.

"Okay. Dear God, bless Faith and help her to come through this surgery healed and unchanged. We pray that it will go well. Please give the surgeons strength and wisdom while working on her. We ask this in Your name, Amen," Gabe prayed as both he and Faith crossed themselves.

Gabe's heart raced.... He knew she'd either come out of surgery changed for the good *or* the bad—maybe not even at all. There were no guarantees. The thought was unbelievable to him. Gabe couldn't bear to lose his dear, sweet Faith.

"I can't believe this.... I hope with all my being that it goes well. I would be heartbroken—I couldn't bear...losing you. You mean too much to me.... Your soul, you've...you've helped me through a lot, you're my philosophical, deep...crazy, devoted Faith. I can't even think of..."

"We'll both keep praying about it," Faith remarked. "If I die, at least I won't be awake for it."

Gabe and Faith chuckled nervously. "No, seriously, I'll be with God. I'm very scared, but I need to feel better. My desire for this oper-ation is stronger than my fear. Faith over fear.... I'll be in God's hands."

"What if I never see you again? Ever?" Gabe asked, his voice shaky.

"I'm scared of that, too," Faith said as Gabe hugged her tightly.

Faith wanted to rejoice as Gabe enveloped her in his arms. Gabe put his chin on her shoulder, gripping her as though she might be ripped away from him.

"It's okay," Faith whispered as Gabe choked up. A few tears rolled down his cheeks as they embraced.

"May I kiss you before you go?" Gabe asked softly.

"What?" Faith asked, shocked. Faith's heart leapt...and at the same time she felt thrilled. Gabe's teary eyes glistened as Faith leaned in.

Gabe brushed his fingertips across her cheek and tilted his head. He gently pressed his lips against hers as he kissed her tenderly. Faith wrapped her arms around his neck and returned his kiss. They closed their eyes as Faith's heart filled with happiness. She got lost in the moment. Her parents were no longer there—she forgot she was in the hospital.

Faith was filled with hope. She felt no fear.

Faith over fear.

EPILOGUE

Four years later

"Goodbye, darling." Mark smiled as he kissed Mary on the cheek and adjusted his cap on his head.

"Goodbye, Mark," Mary called to her husband as she waved from the wooden wrap-around deck.

Mama and Mother, who were talking in the kitchen, echoed their goodbyes.

Several of Mark's siblings were playing in front of the farm-house.

"Goodbye, Papa," said Mary and Mark's oldest child as he padded onto the porch with his two younger siblings following behind him. Dad and John were playing cards as thirteen-year-old Edith dandled Mark and Mary's baby on her lap. Edith handed the baby to Mary.

"Where are your shoes, children? Go back inside and fetch them," Mary instructed as she adjusted the one-year-old baby on her hip. She watched as Mark hefted himself up onto the seat of their wagon and rode away. Mary wrapped an arm around her eldest child—a son. His hair was dark just like Mary's, but curly just like his father's. His eyes were the same gentle blue and bore a warm expression. The three children ran inside to fetch their shoes as the baby nuzzled its head against Mary's chest.

About the Author

Delaney Kraemer was adopted from Guangxi, China and lives in Michigan. She published her first book when she was eleven. Her previous work includes the *German Shepherd Who Howled at the Moon* series.

Delaney's new novel, *Mountains of Our Own*, features a character inspired by her own experiences with epilepsy and CVI (Cortical Visual Impairment). She hopes this book will teach others about epilepsy and the importance of inclusivity.

For more information or to contact the author, visit
http://neurodivergentpublications.com.

Acknowledgments

To Mr. David Aretha, who has always professionally edited my manuscripts, and been very kind to me. He gave me hope that my book could have a broader audience and have an educational impact.

To Dr. Danny McDougall, PhD, CSC, a researcher, educator, and sign language interpreter who specializes in theater interpreting. He is a professor and chair of Sign Language Studies at Madonna University in Metro Detroit, and established the first online resource focused on sign language interpreting for the theater—terptheatre.org. Dr. McDougall gave a plethora of insightful information about Deaf culture.

To Jesse Gordon, my formatter, who is so kind, responsive, skilled, and a blast to work with.

To Martha Bullen, my book marketing consultant. She's generous, gentle, and skillfully led me through the publishing process.

To Jeremy Avenarius, my website designer. He is professional and proficient at his job.

To Alissa Zavalianos, my cover designer, who understood my vision for my cover. She is a great artist, and a sweet person.

To Rebecca Moyer, of Becks Photography, who took my author pictures. She is a talented and kindhearted person.

To momma, Jean Kraemer, for her untiring support.

To my NaiNai, my grandma, Shirley Kraemer, who listened patiently to many read-throughs.

To Auntie Gerry, who died while I was writing this book, who gave advice.

Although my cover went through many changes, I still want to thank Ella Rose King, Tony Varchetti, and Noah Baier, who posed for my original cover.

To my doctors—Dr. Susan Youngs, Dr. Jules Constantinou, and Dr. Andrew Zillgitt—who have been caring for me for many years.

To Karina Cotran, @hearingdifferently, blogger (website is karina cotran.com) and author of the book *Hearing Differently: Growing Up with a Cochlear Implant*, who generously shared information.

To Valli Gideons, author and advocate (@mybattlecall), who provided information about her experience as a parent of deaf children.

To Arij, Bethan, Emilee, Emily, Emily S., Emma, Emmy, Erin, Isabella, Jazzy, Jonathan, Katie, Kimberley, Lauren, Lillian, Natasha, Sienna, and Syd, who educated me about Deaf culture.

REFERENCES

ABC TV & iview. (2019, May 12). People who are deaf answer 'How do you experience music?' | you can't ask that [Video]. YouTube. https://www.youtube.com/watch?v=tTWLoFuEvL4

Academy Originals. (2014, May 19). "Not much to see": How the blind enjoy movies [Video]. YouTube. https://www.youtube.com/watch?time_continue=241&v=QjguIANUEX8&feature=emb_logo

Accidentally Abby. (2017, July 4). Pros and cons of being deaf : A teen's perspective [Video]. YouTube. https://www.youtube.com/watch?v=S6ZCMGKyz4k

Adams, K. (2016, December 15). How to write about depression. Writers Cookbook. https://www.writerscookbook.com/how-to-write-about-depression/.

AJ+. (2018, December 5). What it's like to be deaf | AJ+ [Video]. YouTube. https://www.youtube.com/watch?v=0YcGev7B5AA

Allure. (2016, September 19). Ballerina Lauren Lovette shares her ultimate footcare routine | Allure [Video]. YouTube. https://www.youtube.com/watch?v=-90_mt8jUJ4

American Foundation For The Blind. (n.d). Transcription for page from Nella Braddy Henney's book, 'Anne Sullivan Macy: The story behind Helen Keller.'"

Antique Menswear. (2020, October 26). Q&A with an everyday Edwardian [Video]. YouTube. https://www.youtube.com/watch?v=XmR1wGx0C6Y

Arlen, T. (2014, May 19). The redoubtable Edwardian housemaid and a life of service. Tessa Arlen. http://www.tessaarlen.com/redoubtable-housmaid-life-belowstairs/

ASL Terminology. (n.d). https://www.lifeprint.com/asl101/pages-layout/terminology.htm

Aspinall, A. (2017, February 1). How video chat can transform relationships for people with hearing loss. Hearing Like Me. https://www.hearinglikeme.com/skype-can-transform-relationships-people-hearing-loss/

Asthana, A. (2007, February 3). Historic papers reveal life of Edwardian schoolgirls. The Guardian. https://www.google.com/amp/s/amp.theguardian.com/uk/2007/feb/04/schools.education1

Attitude. (2016, July 26). Parenting with sign language [Video]. YouTube. https://www.youtube.com/watch?v=3iPND6ZTvRs

AwesomenessTV. (2016, November 26). The rules of ballet – auditions day 1 | JOFFREY ELITE EP 1 [Video]. YouTube. https://www.youtube.com/watch?v=HdheoI6Anug

Ballet dictionary. (n.d). American Ballet Theatre. https://www.abt.org/explore/learn/ballet-dictionary/

Ballet Terms. (n.d). Grand Rapids Ballet.
https://grballet.com/about/ballet-terms/

Barbosa, J. (n.d). Ballet terms explained – Ballet Dictionary online.
Learn to Dance. http://www.learntodance.com/online-ballet-dance-lessons/

Barnard, M. (2018, February 14). The do's and don'ts of dating with
hearing loss. Hearing Like Me. https://www.hearinglikeme.com/dos-donts-dating-with-hearing-loss/

Basic Ballet Positions. (n.d). Pittsburgh Ballet Theatre.
https://www.pbt.org/learn-and-engage/resources-audience-members/ballet-101/basic-ballet-positions/#site-wraps

Bass, E. Z. (2012, April 26). Helen Keller in love. Deep South
Magazine. https://deepsouthmag.com/2012/04/26/helen-keller-in-love/

Bauman, D. & Murray, J. J. (2014, November 13). An introduction to
Deaf gain. Psychology Today. https://www.psychologytoday.com/us/blog/deaf-gain/201411/introduction-deaf-gain

Beard, K. (2017, November 9). Not your average dancer: meet the
Deaf dancer defying stereotypes. Dance Spirit.
https://www.dancespirit.com/deaf-dancer-2503983866.html

Beck, E. (2021, December 30). Child labor in the industrial
revolution. Historycrunch.com. History Crunch.
https://www.historycrunch.com/child-labor-in-the-industrial-revolution.html#/

Bella Maes Designs. (2020, December 18). I made victorian cozy clothes — what did **they** wear to get comfy?! — christmas tea gown [Video]. YouTube. https://www.youtube.com/watch?v=9_3425t_k8M

Bellerose, S. How many years of dance or ballet does it take to be a professional? (n.d). Dance Parent 101. https://danceparent101.com/how-many-years-of-dance-or-ballet-does-it-take-to-be-a-professional/

Benson, Nancy & Elliot Stuart (Writers). Elliot Stuart (Director). (2010, December 15). (Season 1, Episode 1.6). [TV series episode]. David Upshal.(Executive Producer). Edwardian farm. Lion Television.

Berke, J. (2020, March 6). The sound of Deaf speech can vary widely. https://www.verywellhealth.com/what-does-deaf-speech-sound-like-1048743

Bernadette Banner. (2020, April 16). Achieving that classic Edwardian shape: reconstructing a 1902 bust bodice [Video]. YouTube. https://www.youtube.com/watch?v=CbzaBr4W4kk

Bernadette Banner. (2020, May 12). I tried following a real Edwardian hair care routine [Video]. YouTube. https://www.youtube.com/watch?v=oek7W5IRAdg

Bernock, D. (n.d). 15 powerful childlike qualities to regain. Danielle Bernock. https://www.daniellebernock.com/15-powerful-childlike-qualities-to-regain/

Berry, J. (2018, July 11). How do I know I am feeling depressed? Medical News Today. https://www.medicalnewstoday.com/articles/314071

Best, C. Meet the matchstick women — the hidden victims of the industrial revolution (2018, March 8). The Conversation. https://theconversation.com/meet-the-matchstick-women-the-hidden-victims-of-the-industrial-revolution-87453

BFI. (2017, February 18). Textiles on film: Preston's cotton industry [Video]. YouTube. https://www.youtube.com/watch?v=3LrEIPxxkew

Biggins, A. (2016, July 5). Ask Anna: Will hearing aids make my hearing go back to "normal"? Hearing Like Me. https://www.hearinglikeme.com/will-hearing-aids-make-my-hearing-go-back-to-normal/

Blakemore, E. (2019, April 9). 'Orphan Trains' brought homeless NYC children to work on farms out west. History. https://www.history.com/news/orphan-trains-childrens-aid-society

Boland, K. (2019, March 21). Why do dancers push through pain even when they know it's bad for them? Dance Magazine. https://www.dancemagazine.com/ignoring-injury-2632161352.html?rebelltitem=5#rebelltitem5

Booth, S. (2015, August 14). Never mind, it's not important. Hearing Like Me. https://www.hearinglikeme.com/never-mind-its-not-important/

Brighton, Butterworth, Grace, Hartford, Paterson, (Executive Producers). New hidden killers. Modern Television and British Broadcasting Corporation.

Brinkman, M. (2020, February 19). What is 'Deaf gain' and 'Deaf identity'? Hearing Like Me. https://www.hearinglikeme.com/what-is-deaf-gain-and-deaf-identity/

Buescher, J. (n.d). Families on the farm. Teaching History. https://www.teachinghistory.org/history-content/ask-a-historian/25754

Burgan, M. (2011). Breaker boys: How a photograph helped end child labor (captured history). Compass Point Books.

Burgess Abramovich, R & Arbuckle, A. (2016, June 5). 1908-1924 Newsies. https://mashable.com/2016/06/05/newsies/

Burke, M. [Molly Burke]. (2016, July 15). Being blind vs. being deaf! [Video]. YouTube. https://www.youtube.com/watch?v=PxPKW04fSoA

Burns, A. (2022, August 9). Railroads in the 20th century, 1900s. American Rails. https://www.american-rails.com/1900s.html

Caspinall, R. (2021, January 20). What not to say to someone with hearing loss. Hearing Like Me. https://www.hearinglikeme.com/supporting-a-loved-one-with-hearing-loss/

Channel 4 Documentaries. (2020, January 28). Exploring horrific working conditions 6-year-olds experienced during the Industrial Revolution. YouTube [Video]. https://www.youtube.com/watch?v=1PmHBqtLFss

Chella Man. (2018, July 1). What happens when Deaf people go to the movies? [Video]. YouTube. https://www.youtube.com/watch?v=qXAuws6uuGM

Child Labor in America. (n.d). Library of Congress.
https://www.loc.gov/classroom-materials/child-labor-in-america/

Child Labor in Factories. (n.d). Manville Schools.
https://www.manvilleschools.org/cms/lib/NJ01912793/Centricity/D
omain/1848/Child%20labor%20in%20factories.docx

Child Labor: Match Girls (n.d). The British Industrial Revolution.
https://britishindustrialrevolution.weebly.com/child-labor-match-
girls.html

Child Labor: The Tortured Hands at the Modernized World. The
Industrial Revolution. (n.d). Mount Holyoke.
https://www.mtholyoke.edu/~hicks22a/classweb/Childlabor/Website
Childlabor/History.html

Child servants during the Victorian era: What jobs did children do
around the house in the Victorian times? (n.d). Fun Kids Live.
https://www.funkidslive.com/learn/really/child-servants-during-the-
victorian-era-what-jobs-did-children-do-around-the-house-in-the-
victorian-times/#

Children in Factories: Conditions and Punishments. (n.d).
http://www.ichistory.com/uploads/1/0/2/9/10290322/conditions_a
nd_punishments_site_2016.pdf

ChoreographyTown. (2016, February 27). Heel dig & ball dig [Video].
YouTube. https://www.youtube.com/watch?v=u3ATXOpgEVg

Chores-Past. (n.d). Grassroots. http://grassroots.pennridge.org/p/p-
chorespast.html

ChrissyCan'tHearYou. (2018, August 15). The reality of lipreading [OC]. [Video]. YouTube. https://www.youtube.com/watch?v=xlGXhGQrrsM

ChrissyCan'tHearYou. (2018, September 8). Dos and don'ts of interacting with the Deaf community [CC] [Video]. YouTube. https://www.youtube.com/watch?v=pDA_EXFTpxo

Classrooms in Victorian and Edwardian schools. (n.d). 1900s.org. https://www.1900s.org.uk/1900s-schools-classrooms.htm

Clearbrook, C. [Cheyanna Clearbrook]. (2019, February 8). My mainstream school experiences [Video]. YouTube. https://m.youtube.com/watch?v=9fLyclcn7Hg

Clearbrook, C. [Cheyenna Clearbrook]. (2019, September 27). My Deaf family/Dossier (CC) [Video]. YouTube. https://www.youtube.com/watch?v=WtVIyObk9Cc

Clearbrook, C. [Cheyenna Clearbrook]. (2020, January 8). Why don't I teach ASL? [Video]. YouTube. https://www.youtube.com/watch?v=vBMF75K-m78

Cloud and Victory. (2020, June 3). Professional ballerina Q&A | Precious Adams, English National Ballet [Video]. YouTube. https://www.youtube.com/watch?v=b3MGLFvq-hA

Cluff, D. B. [David B. Cluff]. (2017, December 17). What does a cochlear implant sound like? [Video]. YouTube. https://www.youtube.com/watch?v=7l-dD4xNk-M

Cochlear Implants. (2012). Cochlear Implants National Cochlear Implant Users Association (NCIUA). Hearing Link. https://www.hearinglink.org/your-hearing/implants/cochlear-implants/

Cochlear Implant Cost. (n.d). Baby Hearing. https://www.babyhearing.org/devices/cochlear-implant-cost

Copeland, Misty. (2016). Life in motion: An unlikely ballerina, Young Readers Edition. Aladdin.

Copeland, Misty. (2017). Ballerina body: Dancing and eating your way to a lighter, stronger, and more Graceful you. Grand Central Life & Style.

Cotran, K. (n.d). How I hear music. Karina Cotran. https://hearingdifferently.com/how-I-hear-music/

Cotran, K. (2018, October 18). My hearing loss is not inspirational. Karina Cotran. https://hearingdifferently.com/my-hearing-loss-is-not-inspirational/

Cotran, K. (2019, November 3). Do I identify as a person with a disability? Karina Cotran. https://hearingdifferently.com/do-I-identify-as-a-person-with-a-disability/

Cotran, K. (2020, July 26). Why I bluff – and why I should stop. Karina Cotran. https://hearingdifferently.com/why-I-bluff-and-why-I-should-stop/

Cotter, J. (2019, July 11). How did people clean their teeth in the olden days? The Conversation. https://theconversation.com/curious-kids-how-did-people-clean-their-teeth-in-the-olden-days-119588

Crow, S. (2020, February 26). 15 subtle but surefire signs you're a pessimist. Best Life. https://bestlifeonline.com/pessimist-signs/

CrowsEyeProductions. (2018, July 24). Getting dressed in WW1 – VAD nurse [Video]. YouTube. https://www.youtube.com/watch?v=QZOaMbTRxWY

CrowsEyeProductions. (2018, September 27). Getting dressed in WW1 – young woman [Video]. YouTube. https://www.youtube.com/watch?v=3GziwpqMZHs

CrowsEyeProductions. (2019, November 29). Getting dressed in 1910s London – working class suffragette [Video]. YouTube. https://www.youtube.com/watch?v=YcBEywxurQA

CymaSpace. (2016, July 6). Deafness + music [Video]. YouTube. https://www.youtube.com/watch?v=c-mf0VGsriQ

Cyr, M. (n.d). Going pro—should I be a professional dancer? Dance Sport Place. https://dancesportplace.com/going-pro-professional-dancer/

CYTSanDiego. (2011, April 19). Heel ball and toe – beginning tap dancing [Video]. YouTube. https://www.youtube.com/watch?feature=share&v=6LdKRN-9YC0&app=desktop

Dancing Career Information: Becoming a Professional Dancer. (2020, January 19). Best Accredited Colleges. https://study.com/articles/Dancing_Career_Information_Becoming_a_Professional_Dancer.html

Darling Videos. (2019, December 18). Edwardian fashion [Video]. YouTube. https://www.youtube.com/watch?v=63bGagNwLHk

Davis, John, & Keller, Helen. (2002). Rebel lives: Helen Keller. Ocean Press.

Deaf Teens: Hearing World on Vimeo. [BSL Zone]. (2015, January 15). BSL zone: Found – documentary about Deaf identity (2015) [Video]. YouTube. https://www.youtube.com/watch?v=vKWBjMYNmwg

Della Santina, C. [Johns Hopkins Medicine]. Introduction to cochlear implantation: Johns Hopkins Cochlear Implant Center | Q&A (2017, April 17). [Video]. YouTube. https://www.youtube.com/watch?time_continue=116&v=0wYUd24x248&feature=emb_logo

DeQuire, K. (2020, April 27). Learning to overcome poor communication habits caused by my hearing loss. Hearing Like Me. https://www.hearinglikeme.com/learning-to-overcome-poor-communication-habits-caused-by-my-hearing-loss/

Do You Have a Fear of Dancing? (2018, February 26). Fred Astaire Franchised Dance Studios.

Dodds, F. (2020, February 12). 10 behaviors people find condescending. Entrepreneur. https://www.entrepreneur.com/article/346238

Dressed In Time. (2020, May 14). Dressing the Edwardian lady [Video]. YouTube. https://www.youtube.com/watch?v=usNkFboiBGA

Druga, M. (2015, November 6). Parenting styles in the 1910s. Melina Druga. https://www.melinadruga.com/parenting-in-1910/

Druga, M. (2016, April 14). Victorian and Edwardian orphans: Nothing like their fictional counterparts. Melina Druga. https://www.melinadruga.com/victorian-and-edwardian-orphans/

Edgar, L. [Lily Edgar]. (2020, August 13). What I eat in a day as a ballerina / professional ballet dancer | Lily Edgar [Video]. YouTube. https://www.youtube.com/watch?v=LlPZCxSaR5c

Edgar, L. [Lily Edgar]. (2020, November 24). What's in my dance bag as a professional ballerina | whats [sic] in my bag | Lily Edgar [Video]. YouTube. https://www.youtube.com/watch?v=scBxC27oGq0

Edgar, L. [Lily Edgar]. (2020, December 21). Vlogmas Day 20! [Video]. YouTube. https://m.youtube.com/watch?v=c1CzMI1cEVY

An Edwardian Dinner Party. (2013, January 8). Brighton Museums. https://brightonmuseums.org.uk/discover/2013/01/08/an-edwardian-dinner-party/

1833 Factory Act: Did It Solve The Problems Of Children In Factories? (n.d). The National Archive. https://www.nationalarchives.gov.uk/education/resources/1833-factory-act/

The 1833 Factory Act. (n.d). UK Parliament. https://www.parliament.uk/about/living-heritage/transformingsociety/livinglearning/19thcentury/overview/factoryact/

Ellen Street. (2017, May 25). Profile of a Deaf dancer [Video]. https://www.youtube.com/watch?v=wym_wxif0C0

Eschner, K. (2017, June 27). Three big ableist myths about the life of Helen Keller. Smithsonian Magazine. https://www.smithsonianmag.com/smart-news/three-big-ableist-myths-about-life-helen-keller-180963793/

ExpertVillage Leaf Group. (2009, July 15). Tap dancing: tap dance: Toe tap [Video]. YouTube. https://www.youtube.com/watch?v=SikBQKjuNJo

Factory Accidents. (n.d). Were factories really bad for children? https://sites.google.com/site/childreninmills/sources

Factory Discipline. (2009, November 12). Industrial Revolution. https://industrialrevolution.wordpress.com/tag/punishment/

The Feed SBS. (2016, May 18). Profoundly deaf hip hop dancer – the feed [Video]. YouTube. https://www.youtube.com/watch?v=9HRLBgHKN1c

Feigel, L. (2015, March 25). Servants: a downstairs view of twentieth-century Britain by Lucy Lethbridge – review. The Guardian. https://www.theguardian.com/books/2013/mar/25/servants-lucy-lethbridge-review

Ferreoiro, E. (2020, January 29). Infographic: Deaf gain, that wonderful idea that is changing the world. Unusual Verse. https://www.unusualverse.com/2020/01/infographic-deaf-gain.html

5 things I wish hearing people would know. (2019, May 14). Hearing Like Me. https://www.hearinglikeme.com/what-you-should-know-about-living-with-hearing-loss/

5 Tips For Dating A Deaf Person. (n.d). Relay South Dakota. https://relaysd.com/news/5-tips-for-dating-a-deaf-person

Fun Kids Learn. (2019, August 23). Jobs around the house (Jobs from the past) [Video]. https://www.youtube.com/watch?v=dS5Rp_8Rgrs&feature=emb_logo

Gentleman's Gazette. (2021, July 12). What men really wore in the 1910s [Video]. YouTube. https://www.youtube.com/watch?v=cL46gZEg3QU

Gentleman's Gazette. (2022, September 2). What men really wore in the 1900s (1900-1909) [Video]. YouTube. https://www.youtube.com/watch?v=bP6N7vLA15Q

Glamour. (2019, December 23). Ballerina masters the Nutcracker's 'sugar plum fairy' in a day | glamour [Video]. YouTube. https://www.youtube.com/watch?v=K97ash4dXs4

Glamour. (2020, July 30). Every exercise pro ballerina Scout Forsythe does in a day | on pointe | glamour [Video]. YouTube. https://www.youtube.com/watch?v=Md2hht2RhJI

Glamour. (2020, November 25). Every item in pro ballerina Scout Forsythe's ballet bag | on pointe | glamour [Video]. YouTube. https://www.youtube.com/watch?v=4yFm9oCEStA&t=198s

Glamour. (2020, December 9). Every ballet myth debunked by ballerina Scout Forsythe | on pointe | glamour [Video]. YouTube. https://www.youtube.com/watch?v=5Nk-YrmZI3k

Glamour. (2021, January 19). Every ballet hairstyle with pro ballerina Scout Forsythe | on pointe | glamour [Video]. YouTube. https://www.youtube.com/watch?v=M2XDQP5caT0

Great Big Story. (2019, January 25). This transgender ballerina is raising the bar [Video]. YouTube. https://www.youtube.com/watch?v=fD_3lUpCTM0

A Guide On How to Select The Appropriate Class/Level For Your Child. (n.d). FNQ Dance Academy. http://www.fnqdanceacademy.com.au/wp-content/uploads/2011/12/FNQDA-2016-pricelist-and-class-guide.pdf

A Guide to Ballet—Glossary. (n.d). City Academy. https://www.city-academy.com/news/a-guide-to-ballet-glossary/

Guth, D. (2020, August 31). How to best communicate with someone with hearing loss. Hearing Like Me. https://www.hearinglikeme.com/communication-tips-for-people-with-hearing-loss/

Guy jones. (2015, June 25). 1900-1901 – victorian and Edwardian workers captured on film (w/ added sound Version 1) [Video]. YouTube. https://www.youtube.com/watch?v=SXxuNncWq4s

Hamlett, J. (n.d). Space and emotional experience in Victorian and Edwardian English public school dormitories. https://link.springer.com/chapter/10.1057/9781137484840_7

Hansan, J. (2011). The American era of child labor. Social Welfare History Project. https://socialwelfare.library.vcu.edu/programs/child-welfarechild-labor/child-labor/

Harrington, K. (n.d). Courtship, love, and intimacy. Rollins Education. https://www.rollins.edu/annie-russell-theatre/documents/upton/upton-abbey-research-courtship.pdf

Haskins, J. (2020, September 4). How to copyright a script. Legal Zoom. https://www.legalzoom.com/articles/how-to-copyright-a-script

Haynes, T. (Director). (2017). Wonderstuck. [Film]. Amazon Studios.

Healthbridgeweb. (2013, April 22). Relay communication services (TTY version) [Video]. YouTube. https://www.youtube.com/watch?v=vsQ73575Qp8

Hearing Like Me—A Hearing Loss Community. (2019, May 14). 5 Things I want hearing people to know. [Video]. YouTube. https://www.youtube.com/watch?v=AulPVEECMS8&t=20s

The History & Etiquette of Afternoon Tea. (n.d). Mathis House. https://www.mathishouse600main.com/tea-history-and-etiquette-of-afternoon-tea.htm

History Crunch. (2022, August 24). Child Labor in the Industrial Revolution – Video infographic. [Video]. YouTube. https://www.youtube.com/watch?v=nN-mmQuyU_8

History Place Child Labor In America 1908-19, 12 Photographs by Lewis Hine. (n.d). The History Place. https://www.historyplace.com/unitedstates/childlabor/index.html

Hoare, J. (2016, January 9). What was school like 100 years ago? How It Works Daily. https://www.howitworksdaily.com/what-was-school-like-100-years-ago/

Housh, E. (2016, March 16). Ballet terms for beginners. Tututix. https://www.tututix.com/ballet-terms-beginners/

How Do Deaf-Blind People Communicate? (2009, February 11). American Association of the Deaf-Blind. http://www.aadb.org/factsheets/db_communications.html

How We Were Taught. (n.d). National Archives. https://www.nationalarchives.gov.uk/education/resources/how-we-were-taught/

Howell, R. [Rodney Howell]. (2009, January 22). Chug tap dance move shown by Rod Howell at unitedtaps.com [Video]. YouTube. https://www.youtube.com/watch?v=1K0vLIPOGaQ

Howell, R. [Rodney Howell]. (2009, February 14). Heel grind time step tap dance move shown by Rod Howell at unitedtaps.com [Video]. YouTube. https://www.youtube.com/watch?v=U0VJomSt2Qo\

Howell, R. [Rodney Howell]. (2009, February 15). Waltz clog tap dance move shown by Rod Howell at unitedtaps.com [Video]. YouTube. https://www.youtube.com/watch?v=UMMeKhQVq1E

Howell, R. [Rodney Howell]. (2014, December 9). Stamp tap dance move shown by Rod Howell [Video]. YouTube. https://www.youtube.com/watch?v=-5krw-ogFl4

Howell, R. [Rodney Howell]. (2014, December 10). Bombershay modern tap dance move shown by Rod Howell [Video]. YouTube. https://www.youtube.com/watch?v=Hhlv9ec3ZxE

Howell, R. [Rodney Howell]. (2014, December 10). Boomerang tap dance move shown by Rod Howell. [Video]. YouTube. https://www.youtube.com/watch?v=Ilmy_P4v2PA

Howell, R. [Rodney Howell]. (2014, December 11). Wings tap dance move shown by Rod Howell [Video]. YouTube. https://www.youtube.com/watch?v=pqQSrCMhrB0

Howell, R. [Rodney Howell]. (2014, December 23). Scuffout tap dance move shown by Rod Howell [Video]. YouTube. https://www.youtube.com/watch?v=8_Eiz1_sfZ4

Howell, R. [Rodney Howell]. (2014, December 25). 5 count wing tap dance move shown by Rod Howell [Video]. YouTube. https://www.youtube.com/watch?v=u0ilLgulIyA

Iliades, C. (2012, September 10). Depression's effect on your appetite. Everyday Health. https://www.everydayhealth.com/hs/major-depression/depressions-effect-on-appetite/

The Industrial Children (n.d.). Museum of Childhood. https://celestetmoc.weebly.com/industrial-revolution-childhoods.html

Industrial Revolution: Child Labor. (n.d). Ducksters. https://www.ducksters.com/history/us_1800s/child_labor_industrial_revolution.php

Inside Edition. Joshua Jack Price and Zoe Lucich. (2020, August 29). Day in the life of professional teen ballet dancers. [Video]. YouTube. https://www.youtube.com/watch?v=7iHj1_6s0b4

Insider. (2018, September 8). How ballerinas customize their pointe shoes [Video]. YouTube. https://www.youtube.com/watch?v=9tISaWeO9q8

Insider. (2018, December 23). The extreme workout regimen of a professional ballerina [Video]. YouTube. https://www.youtube.com/watch?v=EzS0OQzOYjo

Insider. (2019, July 24). Ballet shoes made for brown-skinned ballerinas [Video]. YouTube. https://www.youtube.com/watch?v=dpdhXG0h_Og

Insider. (2019, November 22). Ballerina breaks down 11 iconic ballet scenes | how real is it? [Video]. YouTube. https://www.youtube.com/watch?v=uloBdN4WNkk

Insider. (2020, April 8). Professional ballerina's workout routine while stuck at home (ft. Isabella Boylston) [Video]. YouTube. https://www.youtube.com/watch?v=KVGNa_aR9ys

Insider. (2020, June 18). Ballerina breaks down how to customize pointe shoes | on pointe | glamour [Video]. YouTube. https://www.youtube.com/watch?v=6PtpMaAv6Sc&t=4s

Jackson, K. (2015, October 5). A lesson in Edwardian etiquette. BYU 4th Wall Dramaturgy. https://4thwalldramaturgy.byu.edu/a-lesson-in-edwardian-etiquette

Jane Austen's Edwardian Servants. (n.d). Jane Austen's World. https://janeaustensworld.wordpress.com/tag/edwardian-servants/

Kakareka, J. [Jeanette Kakareka (ballerinaandhome)]. (2020, June 8). What a professional ballerina eats in a day + 5 recipes! [Video]. YouTube. https://www.youtube.com/watch?v=zXnj4-sDyPI

Katie. @Ktnlifts. (2020, October 21). Do's and don'ts when you interact with deaf people. [Video File]. Retrieved from https://www.instagram.com/reel/CGndnbrDXB0/

Katie. @Ktnlifts. (2020, November 5). How to position yourself so we can understand you. [Video File]. Retrieved from https://www.instagram.com/reel/CHN_2Twjku_/

Katie. @Ktnlifts. (2021, January 19). Things you shouldn't say to Deaf people. [Video File]. Retrieved from https://www.instagram.com/reel/CKPHvGfDI4I/

Keaten, O. (2022, February 8). Child Labor Act of 1916. https://www.archives.gov/milestone-documents/keating-owen-child-labor-act

Keller, Helen. (1902). The story of my life. Doubleday, Page & Co.

Keller, Helen. (1903). Optimism. Start Publishing LLC.

Keller, Helen. (1927). Light in my darkness. Doubleday, Page & Company.

Kellgren-Fozard, J. [Jessica Kellgren-Fozard]. (2017, September 16). 13 things my hearing friends should know // International Week of the Deaf [CC] [Video]. YouTube. https://www.youtube.com/watch?v=xQFuL2KYRdc&list=PLhADVL2AiGX-UoiAtnf5_udAB4FMMB5b-&index=5

Kellgren-Fozard, J. [Jessica Kellgren-Fozard]. (2017, September 18). What I can and can't hear // International Week of the Deaf [CC] [Video]. YouTube. https://www.youtube.com/watch?v=6dTq9d9KqmQ&list=PLhADVL2AiGX-UoiAtnf5_udAB4FMMB5b-&index=2

Kellgren-Fozard, J. [Jessica Kellgren-Fozard]. Why I don't sound Deaf // international week of the Deaf [CC] (2017, September 22). [Video]. YouTube. https://www.youtube.com/watch?v=72HS6nTgeOE

Kemp, K. [The Confident Dancer]. (2020, October 5). Becoming a professional ballerina: expectations vs reality | TwinTalksBallet [Video]. YouTube. https://www.youtube.com/watch?v=xS9maZhsPXE

Khan Academy. (2016, August 26). The market revolution – part 1 [Video]. YouTube. https://www.youtube.com/watch?v=KwIQy8xBOsk

King, J. (2018, June 8). To become a professional dancer, how much time should one denote for practicing dance? Quora. https://www.quora.com/To-become-a-professional-dancer-how-much-time-should-one-denote-for-practicing-dance

King, S. (n.d). Fundamentals of ballet. https://www.lbcc.edu/sites/main/files/file-attachments/ballet_terms_ballet_1__2.pdf?1518113825

Kirakosian, M. [MihranTV] (2016, November 11). How to air walk (hip hop dance moves tutorial) [Video]. YouTube. https://www.youtube.com/watch?v=y0mfNWKBQp0&list=RDQMzFkwsspbnls&index=2

Kislik, L. (2017, July 18). Are you tired of being condescended to? Liz Kislik Associates. https://lizkislik.com/tired-of-being-condescended/

Klein, L. (Director). (2001). David Macaulay: Mill times [Film]. WGBH and Unicorn Projects.

Knight, E. & Roth Bittner, K. (2015, December 22). A brief history of toothpaste and the toothbrush. History Undressed. https://www.historyundressed.com/2015/12/a-brief-history-of-toothpaste-and.html

Korstad, R. (1999). Child labor. Ncpedia. https://www.ncpedia.org/textiles/child-labor

KTNV Channel 13 Las Vegas. (2015, July 10). Deaf teen is incredible musician [Video]. YouTube. https://www.youtube.com/watch?v=Jr0wJ7fZIsk

Lamia, M. (2015, March 1). Why bullies don't feel bad (or don't know they do). Psychology Today. https://www.psychologytoday.com/us/blog/intense-emotions-and-strong-feelings/201503/why-bullies-don't-feel-bad-or-don't-know-they-do

Laursen, Michelle S. (2018, April 18). What it takes to become a professional ballerina [Video]. YouTube. https://www.youtube.com/watch?v=9xWtwU7B4no

Lifts and Turns. (n.d). Charleston Ballet. http://www.thecharlestonballet.com/Outreach-Education/Physics-Dance/Lifts-Turns.aspx

Lipscomb, Suzannah (Writer) & Suzanne Phillips (Director). (2013, December 17). The Edwardian home. (Season 1 Episode 2) [TV show episode]. In S. Brighton, J. Butterworth, J. Grace, L. Hartford, C. Paterson (Executive Producers).

Lisk, C. (2015, September 29). When "never mind" goes both ways. Hearing Like Me. https://www.hearinglikeme.com/when-never-mind-goes-both-ways/

Little, B. (2015, September 15). Making toothpaste at home, from ancient times to today. National Geographic. https://www.nationalgeographic.com/news/2016/09/ingredients-toothpaste-science-history/

Love in an Edwardian Country House. (n.d). Hinch House. http://www.hinchhouse.org.uk/ninth/ech.html

Lucy. [Loepsie]. (2016, January 10). The Romanov sisters – tutorial | beauty beacons [Video]. YouTube. https://www.youtube.com/watch?v=xIkMIt2eMWA

Lucy. [Loepsie]. (2016, March 13). Evelyn Nesbit – tutorial | beauty beacons [Video]. YouTube. https://www.youtube.com/watch?v=-AtaVfm55q4

Lucy. [Loepsie]. (2018, June 18). Lucy Honeychurch (A room with a view) | tutorial | beauty beacons of fiction [Video]. YouTube. https://m.youtube.com/watch?v=tmDRsfnaHds

Lucy. [Loepsie]. (2019, October 27). Making an Edwardian hair rat [Video]. YouTube. https://www.youtube.com/watch?app=desktop&v=zWdFE2UbCvA

MacDonald, A. (2018, December 6). Horrible health and safety histories: child labour. Amalgamate. http://www.amalgamate-safety.com/2018/06/12/horrible-health-and-safety-histories-child-labour/

MAGNETFILM. (2020, July 22). Sometimes I dream I'm flying | a young ballerina's life between exhaustion and excitement [Video]. YouTube. https://www.youtube.com/watch?v=nuOtBdghrjY

Mahalodotcom. (2012, April 12). How to tap dance: Shirley Temple [Video]. YouTube. https://www.youtube.com/watch?v=YGIIuOQ8blc

Mahlodotcom. (2012, April 12). How to tap dance: Toe Heels [Video]. YouTube. https://www.youtube.com/watch?v=PuodSJeN1cI

Mahlodotcom. (2012, April 12). How to tap dance: Toe Tap warm up [Video]. YouTube. https://www.youtube.com/watch?v=X61YfjtjjD4

The Many Dangers to Factory Workers. (n.d). http://www.johnsnyderlaw.com/the-many-dangers-to-factory-workers/

Marion, J. (2019, May 9). Is it worth it to become a professional dancer? More Than Dancers. https://www.morethandancers.com/posts/is-it-worth-it-to-become-a-professional-dancer

Marshall, C. [Chrissy]. (2018, September 18). What is concentration fatigue? (with Riki Poynter) [CC] [Video]. YouTube. https://www.youtube.com/watch?v=ZMySYQgd4ps

Marshall, C. [Chrissy]. (2019, July 16). Hearing parents perspective on raising a Deaf child [CC] [Video]. YouTube. https://www.youtube.com/watch?v=jSWPFaZSyWY

Marshall, C. [Chrissy]. (2019, July 30). Rejected everywhere except USC school of cinematic arts [CC] [Video]. YouTube. https://www.youtube.com/watch?v=KlvOJXuBYTA

Martin, H. [HannahMartinRG]. (2020, November 21). a hectic 48 hours in the life of a ballet student [Video]. YouTube. https://www.youtube.com/watch?v=dsiju7QhPIg

Marx R. E. (2008). Uncovering the cause of "phossy jaw" circa 1858 to 1906: oral and maxillofacial surgery closed case files-case closed Journal of oral and maxillofacial surgery. Official journal of the American Association of Oral and Maxillofacial Surgeons. https://pubmed.ncbi.nlm.nih.gov/18940506/

McCarthy, J. (n.d). Textile manufacturing and textile workers. The Encyclopedia of Greater Philadelphia. https://philadelphiaencyclopedia.org/archive/textile-manufacturing-and-textile-workers/

McGuire, K. (2019, February 20). Upping the stakes: how to mentally prepare for your first company audition. Pointe. https://www.pointemagazine.com/upping-the-stakes-how-to-mentally-prepare-for-your-first-company-audition-2627725600.html?rebelltitem=2#rebelltitem2

McKenzie, A. [Alena Mckenzie]. (2019, June 13). Day in the life of a dancer (class, pointe shoes, rehearsal) [Video]. YouTube. https://m.youtube.com/watch?v=jEV38Bpzxlk

Mercurio, M. (2018, December 10). The profound isolation of being a Deaf teen. Medium. https://medium.com/s/for-the-record/just-text-me-isolation-as-a-deaf-teenager-ca9cbd5ad6b8

New York Magazine. (2019, September 26). How NYC ballet's Lauren Lovette gets it done [Video]. YouTube. https://www.youtube.com/watch?v=YeoRMfhyZiA

Nunnery, S. (2016, November 2). 8 communication tips to strengthen relationships. Hearing Like Me. https://www.hearinglikeme.com/communication-tips-to-strengthen-relationships/

OBSERVER. (2017, January 16). What is a professional ballerina looking for in an off-duty shoe? [Video]. YouTube. https://www.youtube.com/watch?v=_Kvhfc4Qnnc

Olson, S. & Canales, L. (2017, September 11). Fitting in when we stand out. Deaf and Hard of Hearing Teens. https://handsandvoices.org/deafhardofhearingchildren/fitting-in-when-we-stand-out/

OnlyGoodTV. (2018, March 13). BalletNext – a Deaf choreographer is combining ASL and ballet into magic [Video]. YouTube. https://www.youtube.com/watch?v=rJPZFVFRcys

Our World Moves. (2013, February 13). Our world moves: ballet dance move – Chasse [Video]. YouTube. https://www.youtube.com/watch?v=UjFbdeKL7lw

Overton, C. (Director). (2017). The silent child. [Drama/Short]. Slick Films.

Padden, Carol & Humphries, Tom. (2005). Inside Deaf culture. Harvard University Press.

Parenting In The 1900s. (n.d). http://parenting1900s.weebly.com Parfitt, E. (2017, January 5). 10 things no one tells you about being a deaf teen. Hearing Like Me. https://www.hearinglikeme.com/what-no-one-tells-you-about-being-a-deaf-teen/ Paterson, K. (2006). Bread and roses. Houghton Mifflin Harcourt.

Paul, C. A. (2017). National Child Labor Committee (NCLC). Social Welfare History Project. https://socialwelfare.library.vcu.edu/programs/child-welfarechild-labor/national-child-labor-committee/

Penn, A. (Director). (1962). The miracle worker (motion picture). Playfilm Productions.

The People: Ellen Beard. (2003). Manor House. https://www.pbs.org/manorhouse/thepeople/ellen_duties.html

Pietrangelo, A. (2020, May 12). Is impulsive behavior a disorder? Healthline. https://www.healthline.com/health/mental-health/impulsive-behavior#risk-factors

Pittsburgh Ballet Theatre. Ballet Vocabulary. (n.d). Pittsburgh Ballet Theatre. https://www.pbt.org/learn-and-engage/resources-audience-members/ballet-101/ballet-vocabulary/

Poynter, R. [Rikki Poynter]. (2017, August 21). What does my Deaf voice sound like? | Rikki Poynter [Video]. YouTube. https://www.youtube.com/watch?v=Pg9xBRbPBlI&vl=en

Poynter, R. [Rikki Poynter]. (2018, September 10). Bias in the Deaf community (American sign language vlog) [Video]. YouTube. https://www.youtube.com/watch?v=8Q3EILcK6EY

Prairie Public. (2016, April 20). The Massachusetts mill workers, Lowell National Historical Park. YouTube [Video]. https://www.youtube.com/watch?v=zSVk6axNHkQ

Pre-professional hours. (n.d). The Ballet Blog. https://www.theballetblog.com/portfolio/pre-professional-hours/

Punishments. (n.d). Were factories that bad for children? https://sites.google.com/site/childreninmills/punishments

Quarry, K. (2018, March 12). 4 tips for writers creating (realistic) characters with depression. The Mighty. https://themighty.com/2018/03/how-to-make-realistic-character-depression/

Really? Deaf people can dance? – Chris Fonseca, the deaf dance teacher (2016, June 7). https://blog.scope.org.uk/2016/06/07/really-deaf-people-can-dance-chris-fonseca-the-deaf-dance-teacher/

Red Bull Elektropedia. (2020, February 18). The sound of bass: how do deaf people experience a party? [Video]. YouTube. https://www.youtube.com/watch?v=D_7RrfYtNa4

Rettner, R. (2010, August 26). Bullies on bullying: why we do it. Live Science. https://www.livescience.com/11163-bullies-bullying.html

Rigby, J. (2012, January 25). How hard is the life of a professional ballet dancer? The Fourcast News. https://www.channel4.com/news/how-hard-is-the-life-of-a-professional-ballet-dancer

Ringo, A. (2013, August 9). Understanding deafness: not everyone wants to be 'fixed.' The Atlantic. https://www.theatlantic.com/health/archive/2013/08/understanding-deafness-not-everyone-wants-to-be-fixed/278527/

Rogers, P. [patricia1959]. (January 20). An old school photograph. https://patricia1957.wordpress.com/tag/edwardian-school/

Rosenberg McKay, D. (2020, August 1). What is a professional dancer? Live About. https://www.thebalancecareers.com/what-is-it-like-to-be-a-professional-dancer-525577

Ryan and Ellen. [Sign Duo]. (2018, December 22). Deaf person in a hearing family part 3 – 5 ways to include Deaf people during the holidays [Video]. YouTube. https://www.youtube.com/watch?v=hbRTUKb1tp0

Ryan and Ellen. [Sign Duo]. (2020, February 27). Deaf man vs. drive thru: they threw away my food! [Video]. YouTube. https://www.youtube.com/watch?v=_gXbWtGAcS8

Sage, H. J. (2018, February 5). The war between capital and labor. http://sageamericanhistory.net/gildedage/topics/capital_labor_immigration.html

Salem, T. (2019, September 11). A writer's guide...to writing a character with depression. Ari Meghlen. https://arimeghlen.co.uk/2019/09/11/a-writers-guide-to-writing-a-character-with-depression/

Schneiderman, M. (2020, August 9). 9 behaviors that make you seem like a condescending jerk. Fatherly. https://www.fatherly.com/love-money/condescending-behavior-signs-help/

Schuman, M. (2017, January). History of child labor in the United States—part 2: the reform movement. https://www.bls.gov/opub/mlr/2017/article/history-of-child-labor-in-the-united-states-part-2-the-reform-movement.htm

Seeker. (2018, August 8). How do cochlear implants work? [Video]. YouTube. https://www.youtube.com/watch?v=2eJao0bY8lE

Setzfand, A. (n.d). Lewis Hine: Focusing the lens on child Labor. https://36152176.weebly.com/early-life-influences.html

Sew Historically. (2015, March 1). Tooth care and tooth powder – Victorian and Edwardian beauty routine and recipes. http://www.sewhistorically.com/1852-tooth-powder-recipes/

Shirinatra. (2020, January 25). 3 ways to create a gibson tuck/roll | hair tutorial. https://www.youtube.com/watch?v=V_fXPXLHJOQ

Sign Duo. (2020, April 16). How a Deaf person can drive [Video]. YouTube. https://www.youtube.com/watch?v=0-mamQEMxzc

Signed With Heart. (2019, October 17). Can you understand my deaf voice? [Video]. YouTube. https://www.youtube.com/watch?v=StcYKdjhwXE

Signs of Depression. (2019, March 21). Healthline. https://www.healthline.com/health/depression/recognizing-symptoms

Simkin, J. (n.d). Punishment in factories. Spartacus Educational. https://spartacus-educational.com/Irpunishments.htm

Simpson, T. (2019, December 8). Day in the life of a ballet dancer [Video]. YouTube. https://www.youtube.com/watch?v=1_bR95Zj-3c

Simpson, T. (2020, February 9). What 2 ballet dancers eat in a day #5 [Video]. YouTube. https://www.youtube.com/watch?v=EFJHqJi6IbU

Slauer, S. (2018, September 4). 25 vintage photos of newspaper boys that show how differently we used to get our news. Insider. https://www.insider.com/vintage-newsboys-2018-8

SlimaksClass. (2011, December 7). Industrial Revolution: spinning mills. YouTube [Video]. https://www.youtube.com/watch?v=ssi6ZXrp2_s

Smith, E. (2019, March 4). How should I start contemporary dance form? Quora. https://www.quora.com/How-can-I-learn-contemporary-dance-by-myself

The Smithsonian. (n.d). Oral care. The Smithsonian. https://www.si.edu/spotlight/health-hygiene-and-beauty/oral-care

Sobiski, E. (2017, September 28). Children's clothing of the 1800s. Our Everyday Life. https://oureverydaylife.com/childrens-clothing-of-the-1800s-12475545.html

Social Security. (n.d). Top names of the 1990s. Social Security. https://www.ssa.gov/oact/babynames/decades/names1990s.html

Sodanca. (2019, May 22). The morning routine of professional ballerina [Video]. YouTube. https://www.youtube.com/watch?v=6LrKtsrD3tM

Sousa, D. (2013, January 30). What echoed through Edwardian Halls. Edwardian Promenade. http://www.edwardianpromenade.com/music/what-echoed-through-edwardian-halls/

Spinning and Weaving. (n.d). North Lanarkshire Council. https://www.culturenlmuseums.co.uk/story/spinning-and-weaving/

Steele, L. (2018, January 26). How child discipline has changed: a brief history. Fatherly. https://www.fatherly.com/parenting/how-child-discipline-has-changed-a-brief-history/

Stereotypes And Misconceptions About Deaf People. (n.d). Deaf Education Worldwide. http://deafeducationworldwide.weebly.com/stereotypes-and-misconceptions-about-deaf-people.html

Strategies for controlling your anger: (2011). Keeping anger in check. American Phycological Association. https://www.apa.org/topics/strategies-controlling-anger

Strike, K. (2017, February 8). The pain of child labor: Amputees and injuries from when life was cheap (1908 – 1924). Flashbak. https://flashbak.com/the-pain-of-child-labor-amputees-and-injuries-from-when-life-was-cheap-1908-1924-373062/

Stroming, A. [Alison Stroming]. (2018, January 4). What I eat in a day as a ballerina | Alison Stroming [Video]. YouTube. https://www.youtube.com/watch?v=-Rdj-qjbHdM

Stump, T. (2018, February 8). Messengers of a cruel society: Lewis Hine's photographs of child telegraph messengers. Another Century. https://anothercenturyblog.wordpress.com/2018/02/08/messengers-of-a-cruel-society-lewis-hines-photographs-of-child-telegraph-messengers/

Tappymom. (2010, February 19). The soft shoe [Video]. YouTube. https://www.youtube.com/watch?v=Lio1IFrKx7Y

Tass, N. (Director). (2000). The miracle worker [Film]. Disney.

Tate, A. (2010, January 18). Dining and dinners. Edwardian Promenade. http://www.edwardianpromenade.com/etiquette/dining-and-dinners/

Tate, A. (2012, March 1). Domestic servants in Edwardian England. Edwardian Promenade. http://www.edwardianpromenade.com/servants-2/domestic-servants-in-edwardian-england/

Teen Depression. (n.d). Mayo Clinic. https://www.mayoclinic.org/diseases-conditions/teen-depression/symptoms-causes/syc-20350985

Teen Vogue. (2016, October 19). Professional ballerina Isabella Boylston's daily routine | teen vogue [Video]. YouTube. https://www.youtube.com/watch?v=JJD1cw-MB1Y

Teen Vogue. (2020, February 24). Teen ballerina's daily routine 1 week before a show | teen vogue [Video]. YouTube. https://www.youtube.com/watch?v=ndbmEEysKQo

10 Ways Deaf People Prove Us Wrong. (n.d). https://takelessons.com/blog/deaf-culture-asl

Tracey, E. (2014, September 25). Vibrations from floor help deaf dance troupe keep time. BBC News. https://www.bbc.com/news/blogs-ouch-29324932

Vaijayanti, P. M. Edwardian Era Children's Life. (n.d). Victorian Era. http://victorian-era.org/edwardian-era-childrens-life.html

Vaijayanti, P. M. (n.d). Scullery maid and her duties, role and salary. Victorian Era. http://victorian-era.org/scullery-maid-duties-role.html

Vanity Fair. (2020, July 20). Professional ballerina reviews ballet scenes, from 'Black Swan' to 'Billy Elliot' | vanity fair [Video]. YouTube. https://www.youtube.com/watch?v=BSQRv1AetxA

Venning, A. (2010, September 17). Britain's child slaves: they started at 4am, lived off acorns and had nails put through their ears for shoddy work. Yet, says a new book, their misery helped forge Britain. Daily Mail. https://www.dailymail.co.uk/news/article-1312764/Britains-child-slaves-New-book-says-misery-helped-forge-Britain.html

Vera, J. (n.d). Child labor in the cotton mill. The Industrial Revolution and Colonialism. https://tirac.weebly.com/child-labor-in-the-cotton-mill.html

Victorian Schools Facts for Children. (n.d). Victorian Children. https://victorianchildren.org/victorian-schools/

Wallis, L. (2012, September 21). Servants: a life below stairs. BBC News. https://www.bbc.com/news/magazine-19544309

Watson, A. D. (2019, January 6). 52 ancestors week one: first Watson to escape from textile mill work. Family Pictures Genealogy. https://www.familypicturesgenealogy.com/post/2019/01/06/52-ancestors-week-one-first-watson-to-escape-from-textile-mill-work

Webb, A. (2018, April 16). Deaf dancer – an interview with ballerina Simone Botha Welgemoed. Siyaflo. https://siyaflo.com/deaf-dancer-an-interview-with-ballerina-simone-botha-welgemoed/

Wee, K. (2019, September 26). The right way to behave on a professional dance job. Backstage. https://www.backstage.com/magazine/article/the-right-way-to-behave-on-a-professional-dance-job-66734/

Weeks, L. (2015, September 8). The mystery of 'elopement epidemics.' NPR. https://www.npr.org/sections/npr-history-dept/2015/09/08/433551894/the-mystery-of-elopement-epidemics

Wehrenberg, M. (2016, April 20). Rumination: a problem in anxiety and depression. Psychology Today. https://www.psychologytoday.com/us/blog/depression-management-techniques/201604/rumination-problem-in-anxiety-and-depression

What Did People Use as Toothbrushes Before They Were Invented and How Did You Clean Your Teeth in Old Times? (n.d). Fun Kids Live. https://www.funkidslive.com/learn/hallux/dentist/what-did-people-use-as-toothbrushes-before-they-were-invented-and-how-did-you-clean-your-teeth-in-old-times/

What Happened to Children During Alcohol Prohibition? (n.d). Schaeffer Library of Drug Policy. http://www.druglibrary.org/prohibitionresults_drinking_by_children.htm

What is Lyrical Dance, and What is the Meaning Behind it? (n.d). Omaha School of Music and Dance. https://www.omahaschoolofmusicanddance.com/our-blog/lyrical-dance-meaning-lessons/

What Jobs Did Children Perform? (n.d). sitesgoogle. https://sites.google.com/site/childlabornctextilemills/Home/day-in-the-life-of-a-mill-child/childrensjobs

Where I Live: Connecticut (n.d). https://www.ctexplored.org/wp-content/uploads/2017/05/WILCT-Child-Labor.pdf

Whipps, J. [Jazzy]. (2018, September 4). What you really want to know about Deaf life | #AskJazzy [Video]. YouTube. https://www.youtube.com/watch?v=KOX4rZB02qg

Whipps, J. [Jazzy]. (2019, May 12). The truth about Deafness | #AskJazzy [Video]. YouTube. https://www.youtube.com/watch?v=PA1FwOYB6_E

Whipps, J. [Jazzy]. (2019, November 5). What it's like in mainstream school being deaf? [Video]. YouTube. https://m.youtube.com/watch?v=HWj5LZCJuLY

Whipps, J. [Jazzy]. (2020, May 6). The reality of Life as a Deaf YouTuber [Video]. YouTube. https://www.youtube.com/watch?v=-_fn5nOvnP0

Why do People Bully? (2020, November 15). Ditch The Label. https://www.ditchthelabel.org/why-do-people-bully/

Wikipedia (n.d). Annie Sullivan. https://en.wikipedia.org/wiki/Anne_Sullivan Wikipedia. (n.d). Glossary of Ballet. https://en.wikipedia.org/wiki/Glossary_of_ballet

Wikipedia. (n.d). Helen Keller: Career, writing and political activities. https://en.wikipedia.org/wiki/Helen_Keller#Political_activities

Wikipedia. (n.d). Helen Keller. https://en.wikipedia.org/wiki/Helen_Keller Wikipedia. (n.d). Tap dance technique. https://en.wikipedia.org/wiki/Tap_dance_technique

Winthrop, E. (2006). Counting on grace. Yearling.

Winthrop, E. (2006, June). Searching for Addie: the story behind the famous photograph. Elizabeth Winthrop. http://elizabethwinthrop.com/wp-content/uploads/ 2010/02/SocialEducation.pdf

WIRED. (2019, July 24). Interpreter breaks down how real-time translation works | wired [Video]. YouTube. https://www.youtube.com/watch?v=twCpijr_GeQ

WIRED. (2019, September 16). Accent expert breaks down 17 actors playing real people | WIRED [Video]. YouTube. https://www.youtube.com/watch?v=_6ohUUzh9kk

Wish Upon a Ballet. (2010, September 2). Chassé [Video]. YouTube. https://www.youtube.com/watch?v=4B0pH7TL8Xc

Working in The Factory. (n.d). Lowcountry Digital History Initiative. https://ldhi.library.cofc.edu/exhibits/show/charlestons-cotton-factory/working-in-the-factory

Writing characters: depression. (2018, October 18). Writing Helpers. https://writinghelpers.tumblr.com/post/65709879583/writing-characters-depression

The Young Bike Messengers Of The South. (n.d). Dusty Old Thing. https://dustyoldthing.com/young-bike-messengers-lewis-hine/

www.ingramcontent.com/pod-product-compliance
Lightning Source LLC
Chambersburg PA
CBHW051521150726
47997CB00001B/334